Your Life, but cooler!

Check out the other books in the
Your Life, but . . . series:

Your Life, but BETTER!

And coming in December 2010:

Your Life, but sweeter!

Your Life, but cooler!

A novel by
CRYSTAL VELASQUEZ

Delacorte Press

All rights reserved. Published in the United States by Delacorte Press, an imprint of Random House Children's Books, a division of Random House, Inc., New York.

Delacorte Press is a registered trademark and the colophon is a trademark of Random House, Inc.

Visit us on the Web! www.randomhouse.com/kids

Educators and librarians, for a variety of teaching tools, visit us at www.randomhouse.com/teachers

Library of Congress Cataloging-in-Publication Data
Velasquez, Crystal.
Your life, but cooler / by Crystal Velasquez. — 1st ed.
p. cm.
Summary: As a middle school girl trying to decide whether to audition for the choir which might perform at Carnegie Hall, the reader determines the outcome of the story by taking personality quizzes interspersed throughout the text.
ISBN 978-0-375-85085-1 (alk. paper) — ISBN 978-0-375-89671-2 (e-book)
1. Plot-your-own-stories. [1. Auditions—Fiction. 2. Singing—Fiction.
3. Interpersonal relations—Fiction. 4. Middle schools—Fiction. 5. Schools—Fiction. 6. Plot-your-own-stories.] I. Title.
PZ7.V4877Yp 2010
[Fic]—dc22
2009050522

The text of this book is set in 11-point Cochin.

Book design by Marci Senders

Printed in the United States of America

10 9 8 7 6 5 4 3 2 1

First Edition

To my mom and dad,
Madelin and Eliezer Velasquez,
the best parents
in the whole world

And to Arielle Crystal Marte,
my best friend's new daughter,
who brought joy to our lives
when we needed it most

Acknowledgments

Once again, I must start by thanking my editor and friend, Stephanie Elliott. As always, you did a wonderful editing job, suggesting all the right things to make the book better. More important, you have made my dreams come true by giving me this opportunity. Thank you isn't enough, but thank you!

Thanks also to editorial assistant Krista Vitola, who told me she couldn't wait to read the second book in the series. You have no idea how good that made me feel! And your help in shaping the story is much appreciated.

A huge thank-you to copy editor Ashley Mason, who did an amazing job fixing all my mistakes and making me look good. Thank you to Tamar Schwartz, managing editor; Marci Senders, designer; Natalia Dextre, production associate; Colleen Fellingham, associate copy chief; Barbara Perris, copy chief; Barbara Greenberg, proofreader; Meg O'Brien, publicist; Alyssa Sheinmel, marketing manager; and the entire Delacorte Press team. I can't tell you how grateful I am to each and every one of you.

Thanks also to Angela Martini, who provided the adorable cover illustrations; Dan Elliott, who did a great job on my author photo; and Maria Flores, who created a Web site for me that I can be proud of.

I would like to thank my family, the most important people in my life. My mother and father, Madelin and Eliezer Velasquez; my brother, Eli Velasquez; my loveable grandparents, Guillermina and David White; my niece and nephew, Jasmine and Eli; their mother, Amanda Topple-Wildig Velasquez, and grandmother, Jean Topple; my cousin Dennis Viera; my great-aunt Maria Quiñones; my cousin David Viera and his wife, Janet Viera, and their son and daughter David and Melissa Viera; my aunt Liz Pacheco; Richard and Maria Santiago, and their kids, Roque and Gabby; Ronnie Santiago and his wife, Lynette, and daughter, Kelsey; my aunt Esther . . . I could go on and on. I have a big, loving family and feel so lucky to have all of you. (Special mention to Jasmine and my mom, who helped brainstorm ideas for this book. It really helped!) And for those we lost last year, my aunts Milca E. Pennulla and Eugenia Kercado, you are always in our hearts.

I also have a ton of close friends who are endlessly supportive and hilarious. (Dereeka, we've been friends for more than twenty years! Ericka, I can't wait to meet your first baby! Tom, thanks for helping me break through the writer's block and for enlisting your four nieces to be my first reviewers. Dionne, Maria, Selena, Diane, Brigitte, Esther, Jeannie, and all my friends from Ballantine—what would I do without you?) I would name all my friends here, but it would take up five pages. It's a great problem to have. Thank you all for making my life better, cooler, and just plain great. I'd like to thank my college creative writing professor, Yesho Atil, for teaching me so much and making me laugh while you were at it. And thank you to Gene Hult and Annemarie Nye, who gave me my first paid writing jobs, and Howard for years of free haircuts.

And finally, thank you to the readers! I really hope you have as much fun reading this book as I had writing it.

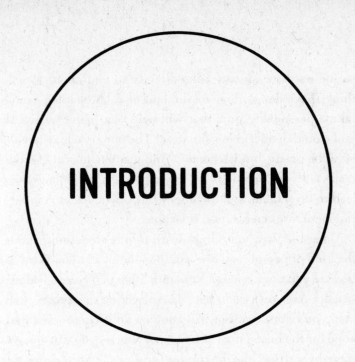

INTRODUCTION

Welcome to *Your Life, but Cooler!* the only interactive series that lets your true personality lead the way! You know what usually happens in these books: the reader gets to the end of a chapter, is faced with a random choice, and is told to decide what he or she wants to happen next. Well, not this time! This book is more like real life.

In this book, it's all about *you*! *You* are the main character, so the narrator always talks directly to you about everything that's happening. At the end of each chapter, you'll take a personality quiz that will help you figure out what you would do in a given situation. The outcome may not always be pretty, but it's honest. And just like in real life, the results of your decisions can be unpredictable. Some roads lead to love, fame, and fortune, while others lead to embarrassment, arguments, and rejection.

Along the way, you might learn a little something about the kind of person you are and the kind of girl you want to be. Are you book smart? Romantic? Do you have a jealous streak? Are you a good friend? Answering the quizzes will help you figure that out. All you can do is be yourself and hope for the best. (If all else fails, of course, you can always start over from the beginning and see where different choices might have led you. That part's a *little* better than real life.)

So go ahead; get started. What would you do on an ordinary day if something extraordinary happened to you? Start reading to find out. It's just like your life . . . but cooler.

Good luck!

chapter ONE

Don't be alarmed. That wailing sound you hear is not an ambulance siren; it's just Mark Bukowski attempting to sing the theme song from *The Little Mermaid*.

"Wandering free, wish I could be part of your wooooooorld . . . ," Mark finishes, raising his arms in a triumphant V while his friends laugh and egg him on. They all seem to be loving the show Mark is putting on in the schoolyard, just outside the main entrance, where everyone gathers before the doors open for homeroom.

Meanwhile, your best friends, Jessie Miller and Lena Saldano, are both covering their ears and wincing as if in real pain. "Now that's just mean," Jessie complains, furrowing her light blond eyebrows.

Lena quickly checks the clock on her BlackBerry. "Seriously! It isn't even eight o'clock yet. Isn't there some law against damaging the eardrums of minors, especially this early in the morning?"

You can't help but smile. "If there isn't, there should be. Good thing I'm not awake enough yet to care," you finish with a yawn, adjusting your backpack on your shoulder. It has already been months since school started, but you're still missing those carefree summer days when you could sleep in until noon if you felt like it. If only school could start at ten or eleven. Or maybe if you could just take your classes over the Internet somehow . . .

Before you have a chance to indulge in your homeschool fantasy, Jessie flicks your temple with two hot pink fingernails.

"Hey! That hurt!" you cry, rubbing your temple.

"Good, maybe it'll wake you up a little. This is no time for you to be half asleep. Today could be major!"

For once, you don't need Jessie to tell you that. After a pretty exciting summer, the school year has been kind of a snoozefest in comparison. But today everybody's buzzing about the choir (which explains Mark's ode to bad singing). According to the flyer that the faculty advisor, Mr. Parker, posted yesterday, they are holding spontaneous auditions this afternoon. It seems your school was chosen to participate in an all-state competition, and the winners get to perform at Carnegie Hall in New York City. (Talk about big time!) Since the choir had been full of eighth graders who all graduated last year, the director is in desperate need of new blood—especially a soloist. The last-minute auditions are designed to find people who can—and will—sing at the drop of a hat, without weeks of practice and preparation.

"Jessie's right," Lena says. "This audition could be historically important. The choir has been too packed to accept any new members for so long, and the eighth graders always got the good solo spots. But now it's wide open! Having lowly fifth, sixth, and seventh graders take over would be a major coup." She clicks open a screen on her BlackBerry and types something with both thumbs.

"And let me guess," you reply, peeking at the screen. "You're going to blog about it, right?"

She shrugs. "Of course. Charlie suggested we do kind of a tag-team blog. He's going to get the teachers' point of view about the choir and music education while I focus on the student body and what they think of the audition process."

It doesn't surprise you at all that Lena has teamed up

with Charlie Daniels. Not only is he just as much of an overachiever as Lena (he even wears ties to school!) but you suspect Lena has a little crush on him. Not that she would admit that in a gazillion years.

"Does that mean you're auditioning too?" a squeaky voice chimes in behind Lena.

You all turn to see Amy Choi standing there, her straight black hair swinging as she looks at each of you excitedly. You can only hope she didn't overhear you say anything you don't want blabbed all over town. Amy considers herself the TMZ of your school. She never met a rumor she didn't like, and she definitely isn't above using her videophone to catch you doing something embarrassing and then posting it on YouTube.

"Not me," Lena answers immediately. "Journalistic principle and all. I can't report on the story and be a part of it too."

You and Jessie share a look while trying to hold back your smiles. You know you're both thinking the same thing. *Sure, Lena. That's why you don't want to audition.* You're pretty sure it has more to do with the fact that over the summer, Amy videotaped Lena hurling into a trash can in the mall. For a while, that YouTube clip got more hits than the one of the baby dancing to Beyoncé's "Single Ladies" video. Since then, Lena has been trying to lie low, not that you blame her.

"Just as well," Amy says with a shrug of her shoulders.

Lena carefully tucks her thick brown hair behind one ear. "What's that supposed to mean?"

Amy sighs and rolls her eyes as if to say, *Don't you know anything?* "For starters, they're going to be looking for singers who are really serious about performing because . . ." Amy looks to her left and then her right and then leans in close, as if she is about to drop a humongous secret. You find yourself leaning in too. "The producers of that show *Glee* might attend the Carnegie Hall performance, looking for extras."

You and your friends immediately lean back and give a synchronized eye roll. You don't even have to say a word. Your smirk and crossed arms say it all. Yeah, right. The producers of a major TV show are going to be cruising for talent from your podunk town. Fat chance.

Amy, seeing the disbelief on your face, prissily adjusts her Hello Kitty messenger bag on her shoulder and purses her lips. "Fine, don't believe me. But look around. You really think even the jocks would be getting ready to audition if it weren't true?"

Hmm . . . She's got a point. As you take a quick look around the schoolyard, it becomes instantly obvious that singing fever has infiltrated every single clique there is: the popular kids, the jocks, the brainiacs, even your little group of indefinables. (When Lena advised you that "indefinables" is not technically a word, your crush—and now friend—Jimmy Morehouse responded that made up or not, nothing else quite describes your merry band of misfits.) Everywhere you turn, kids are standing in tightly huddled groups practicing scales or singing along with their iPods. Melanie from the cheerleading crew is carrying a pom-pom in one hand and sheet music in the other. You bet even Mona Winston, the queen of the popular girls—and your sworn enemy—is warming up her pipes somewhere. (Though you hope her busy modeling schedule will keep her away. Mona has never liked you, so you usually try to steer clear of her if you can.)

If Jimmy didn't already have an art exhibit to worry about, he'd probably be out here too, singing "Do-Re-Mi" instead of getting to the art room super-early to do some last-minute painting. It's hard to believe that you and Jimmy have become close enough friends that he actually called you last night to invite you to the local community center's art show to see his work after school. But he totally did. (This is a huge leap forward, considering that a mere two months ago you barely had the guts to say hi to each other.) And adorably, he even dropped the phone a few times. Sure, that could have just been him being his usual klutzy self, but you prefer to think it was because he was really nervous when he asked you—as if there were any possible way you would say no! Naturally, you promised to come out and support him.

But let's get back to the matter at hand. You hate that you have absolutely no retort for busybody Amy. Could what she's saying be . . . true? Your doubt must be obvious, because Amy gives you a happy little "Mm-hm!" and turns her attention back to your friend. "Besides, no offense, Lena, but the solo spots always, always, *always* go to the

A-listers. Just like everything else." To be fair to Amy, you know she isn't actually trying to be mean. In fact, there isn't a drop of malice in her voice as she says this. She is simply stating it as a fact, as if she had just said "Pizza tastes good" or "Mona Winston is evil"—neither of which anyone in his or her right mind could argue with.

Still, Lena has to object. "But they can't barge in and take over the top spots this time. The faculty judges choosing the soloists are supposed to be unbiased."

Amy sighs deeply and shakes her head. "Didn't you even read the flyer? They're looking for student judges too—to get 'real kids' opinions' or something. They're looking for a soloist who can really connect with kids, not just win over adults. And who do you think is going to sign up to be a judge?" She nods slyly over at Lisa Topple and Maria Santos, two of Mona's most loyal cronies. You've heard that Lisa is only loyal because she wants to use Mona's modeling connections to become an actress. Maria transferred to your school around the same time as Mona, so you guess they bonded over being the new girls. Maria doesn't seem to really like Mona—no surprise there—but being her friend does come with some perks, like meeting the occasional celebrity. And Maria is the type of kid who doesn't necessarily crave the spotlight, but she'll do whatever she can to make sure her friend gets it.

Her point made, Amy flounces away to talk to Lisa and Maria. You open your mouth to protest, but no sound comes out at all. As much as you hate to admit it, Amy is right. The popular kids *do* always get the solos, and they're the captains of all the sports teams and usually get all the leads in the plays. So unfair!

Looking over at Jessie and her furrowed brows, you can tell that the same thought is dawning on her. Only, her sky blue eyes are twinkling and the beginning of a smile is curling her gloss-covered lips. That can mean only one thing: She's got a plan.

"Girls," she says, throwing her arms around your and Lena's shoulders so that you three form a huddle of your own, "Amy is telling the truth. You realize what this means, right?"

"Yeah," you offer in mock disbelief. "If the Queen of Gossip is right, it means all the other gossip rags might be right sometimes . . . and I might have to actually start believing all those *Enquirer* articles! So Megan Fox really *is* an alien!"

Lena giggles, but Jessie just gives you an exasperated sigh. "Maybe, but that's not where I was going. It means yeah, the popular kids rule the school, but maybe that's only because we sit back and let them. We have a real chance with this choir thing to shake things up!"

Lena is no longer giggling. You can tell that Jessie has just tapped into her inner social activist. "A call to action?" Lena says, arching one eyebrow. "I'm intrigued. Go on."

"Well, for starters, I'm going to get the most unlikely kids in school to audition. Who knows what kind of talent has been hiding out in the bio lab and goth club? I can even glam them up a little if they want." Jessie nods at Lena.

"And how about you and Charlie focus your blog on making sure everything stays fair?"

Lena nods enthusiastically as she furiously types into her BlackBerry. "Charlie's going to love that angle. We'd be honored to do our part for justice!"

Jessie smiles a brilliant smile, flashing all her teeth. "Great! That just leaves one crucial part of the plan: our secret weapon."

"What's that?" you ask just as the bell rings and people start shuffling into the building, heading for homeroom.

This time it's Jessie and Lena who share a knowing look before Jessie says, "Duuuh. You! You've just got to go for the solo spot! They're only picking one for the competition piece. I've heard you sing and you would put Christina Aguilera to shame."

You have to admit you're a big shower singer, and, well . . . you have kind of a nice voice. Okay, a great voice. And you totally have a fantasy of singing on top of a car in the middle of New York City, à la Taylor Swift during the MTV Video Music Awards. But fantasizing about singing in front of the whole world and actually doing it are very, very different things.

"I don't know," you mutter hesitantly as you walk into your homeroom class, taking a seat behind Mary McCullen and Holly Deever—who everyone calls Mary Sunshine and Holly Happy-Go-Lucky behind their backs since they are the two gloomiest girls ever.

"You don't know what?" Mary butts in, turning around

in her seat to face you, her stringy black hair clinging to one cheek. Holly, sitting in the seat in front of Mary, turns around too. Looking at their matching black T-shirts, black jeans, and black sneakers, you'd swear they called each other in the morning to coordinate their looks.

> *Holly: How about the gray T-shirts*
> *   today?*
> *Mary: Nuh-uh. That's waaay too*
> *   cheerful.*
> *Holly: Um . . . black again?*
> *Mary: Now you're talking. And don't*
> *   forget to look like your dog just died*
> *   all day.*
> *Holly: Got it.*

If it weren't for the fact that Holly has deep chestnut brown hair and is about five inches shorter than Mary, you'd have trouble telling them apart.

Jessie, sitting to your left, speaks up first. "She doesn't know if she wants to be the next Britney Spears or not."

"She doesn't know if she wants to revolutionize the world by auditioning, or if she should just sit on the sidelines and watch," Lena adds from her seat to the right of you. You suddenly find yourself missing Lena's Shakespeare phase, when she was quoting the Bard every chance she got. Now that she's thinking of joining the school paper (to add to her future college applications, of course), she's been reading every newspaper she can get her hands on, and seems to think every little incident could be a huge world event.

You look at each of your BFFs and shake your head. "Jeez, drama queens. It's not that serious. We're just talking about the choir."

"Pfft," Mary grunts. "The choir auditions? Please. That's so lame."

"Superlame," Holly agrees. "All those people sitting there and judging you? No thanks." They turn in unison to face the front of the class.

"Don't listen to them," Jessie whispers to you. "They think *everything* is lame."

This is true. But they also kind of have a point. You don't mind singing in the shower, but up on a big stage, with a bunch of people staring at you? Um . . . that you'll have to think about. Not that you have time to do that, of course. Already your homeroom teacher, Ms. Campbell (nickname: Mm-mm Soup), is walking in and sighing as she drops her bags on her oversize desk.

"All right, kids," she begins, clapping her hands several times to get everyone to quiet down. "I suppose you all know about the choir auditions taking place this afternoon. Please be advised that this should *not* take away from your class time today. This is not *High School Musical*. There will be no singing in the cafeteria, and certainly no dancing in the streets, understood?" Everyone giggles and looks around at one another, which only frustrates poor Ms. Campbell even more. "But for those of you who want to audition or sign up to be student judges, the sign-up sheets are posted in the hallway outside. They will be there right up until auditions begin, but you have exactly fifteen minutes right now to go and sign your names. Anyone not back here before the bell rings will get detention. Understood?" (She always checks to make sure you understand, just in case you have suddenly forgotten how to speak English.)

But you all know the routine when it comes to her. "Yeees, Mssss. Caaaampbellll," you all recite slowly.

She gives a quick nod and sits down behind the desk, opening her newspaper and taking a sip of her coffee. "Fine. You may go."

The sentence is barely out of her mouth when kids start scrambling for the door. But your butt is still firmly planted in your seat, and Jessie is practically staring a hole into your head. If you go sign your name, there's a good possibility that you'll make a total fool of yourself in front of everybody. But if you don't, you'll be letting Jessie down, not to mention ruining her plan to put a halt to the popular kids' hold on everything. Hello, Rock. Meet Hard Place.

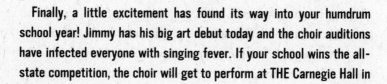

Finally, a little excitement has found its way into your humdrum school year! Jimmy has his big art debut today and the choir auditions have infected everyone with singing fever. If your school wins the all-state competition, the choir will get to perform at THE Carnegie Hall in

New York City! Not to mention that according to only barely reliable sources (Amy Choi), the producers of *Glee* will be there looking for extras for the show. On top of that, you and your friends have an ingenious plan to shake up the social hierarchy of the whole school! Only, you don't seem too willing to do your part. Sure, you could live out your rock-star fantasy and audition—but you could also sit this one out, or at least stick to the judges' table, where it's safe. (Better to judge than be judged, right?) Either way, you've got to decide quickly because homeroom is almost over. It's the moment of truth.

So what's it gonna be? Still not sure? Maybe the following quiz will help you figure it out.

QUIZ TIME!

Circle your answers and tally up the points at the end.

1. In the horror movie you're watching with your friends, the main character, Shelly, is house-sitting for a neighbor. She is watching TV in the living room when she hears a loud thud upstairs. If you were Shelly, you would:

    A. grab a bat and go upstairs to investigate. After all, it's your job to protect the house against burglars, monsters, or whatever is up there!

    B. do your best to remain calm while you call the police and ask them to come check it out. Maybe it's nothing, but you'll let the professionals find out for sure.

    C. run out of there ASAP and call the cops from your place. Oprah Winfrey couldn't pay you enough to stay in that house a second longer than you have to.

13

D. crawl into the nearest closet and curl up into a fetal position. Yes, calling the cops would be a great idea . . . if only you weren't too petrified to move.

2. **You're on vacation in Hawaii and everyone in your tour group is taking turns jumping from a pretty high cliff into the waters below. When your turn comes, you:**

    A. take a running leap off the cliff, shouting "Cowabunga!" as you go into a graceful swan dive. Nothing beats that rush of adrenaline as you go sailing through the air.

    B. are a little nervous. (For some reason the water looks like it's getting farther and farther away the longer you stand there.) But you manage to screw up your courage and cannonball yourself into the water.

    C. practically hyperventilate your way into unconsciousness. Have your fellow travelers not noticed how ridiculously high this cliff is? You opt to find a much lower ledge so you can slip into the water without having a major heart attack.

    D. pretend you don't know how to swim. No way are you jumping from that height! Besides, there could be sharks in the water. You'll stay on land, where it's safe, thanks.

3. **You're on your school's blog, reading a review of your favorite show. The reviewer hates it, and so do all the kids who left comments in the forum. Someone has to be the brave soul who defends what is quite possibly the best show in the history of the world. So you:**

A. write up a brilliant defense of the show and sign your real name. You love the show and you don't care who knows it!

B. defend your show, but sign it with your initials. Your friends will know it's you, but you'll still be anonymous to the rest of the kids.

C. halfheartedly explain why everyone should give the show a chance, and then use a pseudonym. Someone you know might read what you wrote, and there's no need to make yourself a target for ridicule.

D. keep quiet and hope that someone else eventually agrees with you. If no one does, you'll have to make a mental note to keep your love for the show top secret.

4. **It's the last day of school and the boy you have a crush on is about to leave the building. If you don't do something now, you won't see him all summer. So naturally you:**

A. walk right up to him and tell him that you'd really like to hang out sometime. You even come up with a plan for the following week.

B. catch up to him and tell him you hope he has a great summer, then make sure he knows that you'll be home all summer too. Maybe if you hint around enough, he'll ask you to do something with him.

C. blurt out, "Bye, have a great summer!" as you fly past him in the hall. Hey, you're amazed you got that much out!

D. avoid him at all costs. If you make eye contact, he might think you like him. (The horror!)

5. You just got your grades for the semester and, well . . . let's just say you aren't going to be hanging this report card on the refrigerator. Your parents are going to hit the roof when they see it. What do you do?

A. Show it to them right away and prepare for the worst. They have to sign it anyway, so you might as well get it over with and take your lumps now.

B. Make them a great dinner, clean your room, take out the garbage, and make them a card telling them how much you love them . . . and *then* show them your report card. They couldn't possibly get mad while eating your world-famous mac and cheese, right?

C. Right before you leave for school the next day, you put the report card on the kitchen table, where they're sure to see it, with a note asking them to sign it. You're pretty sure they'll cool off by the time you get home. But you definitely don't want to be around when they first read it!

D. Try your hardest to get your dog to eat your report card. Anything beats having to show it to your folks!

Give yourself 1 point for every time you answered **A**, 2 points for every **B**, 3 points for every **C**, and 4 points for every **D**.

—If you scored between 5 and 12, go to page 27.

—If you scored between 13 and 20, go to page 17.

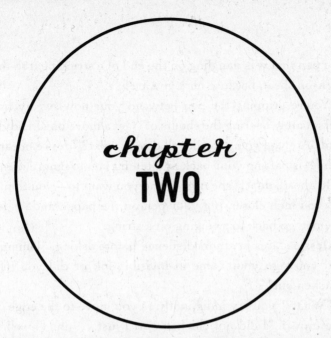

chapter
TWO

Life can be pretty scary. And no one seems to know that better than you. When a dangerous situation pops up—whether it's a bad report card or a burglar creeping around the house—your first instinct is to run away. The good news is, in some cases, running away is absolutely the right response. (The police force exists for a reason!) But sometimes the only way to overcome a fear is by facing it head on. Once you do, you might find life to be a little less scary and a lot more fun.

You don't quite remember walking out of the classroom, but you must have. Some time after you told Jessie you guessed you could sing "You Belong with Me" by Taylor Swift, you must have made your way down the hall and through the crowd. Then you must have picked up the pen that was dangling on the end of a string next to the sign-up sheet, because here you are!

You're gripping the pen between your now-sweaty fingers, barely hearing the shouts of "Get a move on already!" and "Are you going to take all day or what?" Jessie, meanwhile, is patting your back and telling you to ignore them. "Go ahead, do it!" she urges. And you want to—you think. So you inch closer, put your pen on the paper, and . . . let the pen go back to swinging on a string.

Jessie stares in stunned silence before asking, "Ummm, did you sign your name in invisible ink or did you just chicken out?"

"What?" you cry indignantly as you move to the edge of the crowd. "I did not chicken out. I just . . . uh . . . well, I don't want people to think I'm conceited."

Lena, who followed you out into the hall, is now standing beside you with a puzzled look on her face. "Why would anyone think you're conceited?"

"Aw, come on, guys. First I think I can be a model, and now I want to be the main attraction in the choir too?"

Okay, that part is not a total lie. Over the summer you were approached in the middle of the mall by a major model scout, and word of your shot at fame did make its way around school. But that isn't really why you backed out of the choir audition. The truth is, the thought of singing in front of all those people has you scared silly. It's easy to sit at home watching *American Idol* and say that you would have done way better than those contestants. But if you really had to go up there in front of Randy, Kara, Ellen, and worst of all, Simon—not to mention the entire TV-viewing world—you doubt you'd be able to get out even one note.

Sometimes you wish Jessie and Lena didn't know you quite so well, because they can see the truth written all over your face. And you can see disappointment written all over theirs.

"Are you sure?" Jessie asks hopefully. "You're really good. You could be the next Rihanna, the next Miley, the next—"

"I'm sure!" you cut in. Who knows how long Jessie would have gone on with the list of pop princesses?

Jessie sighs and you can see her body deflate a little, like a balloon. "I guess that's that." But then the twinkle in her eye comes back as she glances over at Lena. "Unless . . ."

"Forget it, blondie," Lena snaps, reading Jessie's mind. "I already told you: I can't audition because of journalistic principle." Well, there's that, and the fact that even when she sings "Happy Birthday" people beg her to stop.

"Fine," Jessie says, a note of determination entering her voice. "Someone has to represent our tribe of misfits. So I guess it's going to be me!"

Before you even have time to react, Jessie pushes her way past Jasmine Viera, Kevin Minks, and Lizette Tores (all of whom are signing up to audition), and signs her name in giant curly letters. As she comes back through the crowd, you can see her chest swell with pride and a huge smile spread over her face. She looks so excited; it kind of makes you wish you had had the guts to go for it too. But since you didn't, supporting Jessie is the next best thing.

"Awesome!" you yell, hugging her with all your might. "I'm so proud of you!"

"Me too," Lena says. "This will be a great twist for the blog. I've gotta go tell Charlie!"

As Lena heads back into the classroom to find her blog partner, you continue to congratulate Jessie.

"This is really cool, Jess. I'm glad the plan wasn't ruined because of me. Superfashionista to the rescue!"

Jessie laughs, plants her fists on her hips, and spreads her legs in a V, in a Wonder Woman stance. "That's me: saving the world one fabulicious song at a time."

You giggle happily. "So, what are you going to sing anyway?"

Jessie's superhero persona falters for a second and she turns back into the eighth grader you know and love. "Oh, umm . . . I hadn't really thought about that." After staring at the ceiling for a few moments while drumming her fingers against her chin, she says, "Hey! I'll just sing the song you were going to sing before you . . . uh . . ."

"Chickened out?" you offer, a touch of shame in your voice.

Jessie holds her hands up in the air as if to say, *Don't shoot!* "I didn't say that," she pleads.

You shrug miserably. "It's okay. You can say it. I guess that's what I did."

Jessie reaches out and gently squeezes your shoulder. "Listen, if it makes you feel any better, you would have been no match for my superhot vocal stylings anyway."

Her voice is serious and sympathetic, but you know she's kidding just to make you smile, which works, of course.

"Oh, is that so, you wannabe Britney Spears?" You playfully shove Jessie's left shoulder.

She gasps as if she's shocked by your moxie. "Yeah, that's so!" She shoves you back, both of you giggling now.

"All right," you say, "then let's hear a sample, shall we? Blow me away."

Jessie looks around self-consciously. "What, right here? Now?"

"Why not? You're going to have to do it later anyway. You might as well get used to an audience of one first. Besides, those guys aren't paying us any attention," you point out, nodding at the crowd still swarming around the sign-up sheets, shouting for their turn with the pen. Lena must be rubbing off on you, because that was downright logical.

Unable to argue with the truth, Jessie shrugs, turns on her megawatt smile, and says, "All right. Prepare to be blown away." She clears her throat and starts belting out the chorus of "You Belong with Me."

But when the lyrics start coming out of her mouth, you can't tell if she's still joking or not. You really hope so, because *it's awful*! Beyond awful! Jessie is really giving

Mark Bukowski a run for his money in the bad singing department. She's having trouble hitting those high notes, so instead of singing them she's screaming them, making you wish you had a set of earplugs on you. Good thing she has her eyes closed the whole time, so she can't see the horrified look on your face.

When she finally stops, you scramble to set your expression back to neutral.

"So? What did you think?" she asks breathlessly. "Pretty great, right?"

Haven't fifteen minutes gone by yet? Where on earth is the end-of-homeroom bell when you need it?

There's good news and there's bad news. Let's cover the bad news first, to get it out of the way. You can call it what you want, but the truth is, you chickened out of the audition. So say good-bye to singing in Carnegie Hall (or on *Glee*). Plus, you won't be doing your part to make sure the popular kids don't dominate the choir like they rule everything else. The good news is, your buddy Jessie has agreed to pick up your slack and go for a solo. Hooray! Oh, but wait . . . there's more bad news! What Jessie calls singing sounds a lot more like screeching. Had it been an *American Idol* audition, Simon Cowell would have said something crushing and sent her packing. But you can't tell Jessie that, can you? Take the quiz to see if you're willing to deliver the awful truth.

QUIZ TIME!

Circle your answers and tally up the points at the end.

1. **It's the first day of school after summer vacation. Everybody is talking about all the cool places they went over the summer. But the farthest you got was your aunt Edna's, where you helped clean out all the junk in her closets for a garage sale. *So* not cool. When someone asks you what you did all summer, you say:**

    A. "I had to hang out at my aunt's house and help with the garage sale. Pretty lame, right?" No use lying. If someone from school saw you manning your aunt's old boot collection, they'd be sure to expose you. Then you'd be twice as embarrassed! And if you acknowledge the lameness first, you beat everybody else to the punch.

    B. "Nothing as cool as what you did. Tell me more about your trip to Disney World. . . ." Rather than reveal the sad truth, you just change the subject. No one can give you grief about your so-called summer vacation if they're too busy telling you about theirs.

    C. "I spent the summer learning about antiques, sales, and dealing with the public from a prominent member of the community. Since I want to be a businessperson someday, I figured I should start learning now!" Hey, that's kinda true—if you think of your aunt's Frisbee collection as "antique."

    D. "I spent the summer at the NASA space camp in Alabama, learning how to walk in zero gravity." Okay, maybe you didn't, but who's gonna know? Besides, you did watch that movie *Apollo 13* on TV. Close enough.

2. **Your mom has put on a little weight lately, so she's going shopping to buy some new pants. She takes you along because she values your opinion. When she tries on the first pair, she asks if you think they make her look fat. Your answer?**

   A. You're completely honest and tell her that they do make her look a little frumpy. You don't want your mom walking around in those things thinking she looks good—especially when she picks you up at school!

   B. Instead of answering, you immediately grab a different pair that you're sure will be a better fit and hand them to her without a word. In this case, silence speaks volumes.

   C. Fudge the truth by saying no, but that the color is all wrong. Yes, the first pair looked terrible on her, but she doesn't need to know that.

   D. You tell your mom she looks like a supermodel in those pants. They look great on her! That may not be true, but you don't want to hurt her feelings.

3. **Your grandmother gave you a sweater for your birthday last week, and she's on her way over for dinner. You know she's expecting you to wear the new sweater. Unfortunately, it's so hideous that you could use it as a Halloween costume. You were planning to let it gather dust in your closet. But what do you do when she gets to your house?**

A. Give the sweater back to your grandmother, telling her you know she meant well, but what was she thinking? The front had a unicorn, rhinestones, and sequins on it. Not your style at all. You hope she kept the receipt.

B. Thank her for buying you a gift, but confess that you're a little old for unicorns now. You don't want to upset her, but you also don't want a closet full of rainbows and rhinestones. If you tell her the truth now, maybe she'll switch over to cooler stuff.

C. Wear the sweater to dinner, claiming that you love it, but toss it as soon as your grandmother leaves. You don't want her to know you didn't like it, but you also can't be seen in public in that thing!

D. Tell her you lost the sweater in some freak windstorm. For all you know it's floating out over the ocean by now and you're heartbroken! (Careful not to lay it on too thick, though, or she might buy you another one just like it.)

4. **The boy you have a crush on has finally asked you to go see a movie with him. Too bad he wants to see a cheesy comedy that you have zero interest in. What do you do?**

A. Admit that you're really not into seeing the comedy. But you'd still love to hang. Maybe you can go play miniature golf instead?

B. Subtly nudge him toward seeing the blockbuster that just came out. That movie still wouldn't be your first choice, but it beats two hours of bathroom humor any day.

C. Lie and say you've already seen it, and then drag him to see any other movie that's showing.

D. Go see the flick he wants to see and pretend you love it (even though you're inwardly cringing through every unfunny minute).

5. **A good friend of yours has just started dating a guy that you happen to know is a big fat jerk. After she finishes gushing, she asks you point-blank what you think of him. You say:**

A. "Honestly? You could do a lot better." She might not want to hear that, but if she doesn't want your honest opinion, she shouldn't have asked.

B. "He's okay, I guess. He didn't make a great first impression on me, but maybe I just need to get to know him better." After all, if your friend likes him this much, he must have a good side *some*where.

C. "I don't really know him." That isn't altogether true, but having to tell your friend what you really think would be even worse than spending a day with her obnoxious new guy.

D. "He's awesome! I'm so happy for you!" You hate lying to her, but you're just trying to be supportive. Besides, she'll keep dating him no matter what you say, so why make her feel bad about it?

Give yourself 1 point for every time you answered **A**, 2 points for every **B**, 3 points for every **C**, and 4 points for every **D**.

—If you scored between 5 and 12, go to page 36.

—If you scored between 13 and 20, go to page 45.

chapter
THREE

Brave girl! You understand that courage doesn't mean you never feel afraid, but that you don't let your fears get the best of you. You would make an awesome firefighter, police officer, or stuntwoman. And in your day-to-day life, you face down some pretty scary situations. Just remember to use your common sense to recognize when you should listen to your fear and let it guide you to safety. (Even firefighters know when it's time to leave the building and call for backup.)

E ven though your nerves are bouncing all over the place like balls in a pinball machine, you screw up your courage and walk confidently into the hallway. Already there is quite a crowd surrounding the sign-up sheets. Lizette Tores, Jasmine Viera, and Mark Bukowski are among the kids vying to get closer. Seeing all your possible competition gives you pause for a moment. Can you really do this?

Just when you feel like you might want to turn and run, Jessie pats you on the back encouragingly. And Lena gives you a big thumbs-up. They obviously believe in you. And then you think about Jimmy, who is brave enough to show his artwork to the whole neighborhood—which might as well be the whole world. If he can do that, you can definitely do this.

Without any further hesitation, you make your way through the crowd, grab the pen that is swinging from a string next to the bulletin board, and sign your name in big capital letters right under Jasmine's. There. No backing out now!

"Sweet!" Jessie cries, clapping. "You've got guts, my friend!"

Lena and Charlie appear on the other side of you, clapping along. "Bold move!" Charlie agrees.

"Yeah, thanks," you mutter, "but right now I'm not feeling too bold." You grab your stomach, suddenly downright nauseated. "What was I thinking? I'm going to be at the audition all alone!"

Jessie bites her lip, something she tends to do right before she makes a big decision. "Not alone," she says brightly, grabbing your hand and pulling you back through the crowd to the sign-up sheets, just beating Lizette to the pen.

"Hey!" Lizette cries, flipping her curly black hair over her shoulder. "I was about to use that, you know."

"Sorry, Lizette," Jessie calls. "But I'm on a moral-support mission." With that, she takes the pen and signs her name in a fancy flourish right under yours.

When she turns around to see your jaw unhinged in total shock, she shrugs as if what she did was no big deal at all. "Eh, it's the least I could do for the girl who always shared her M&M'S in second grade. Besides, it'll be way easier for me to convince other kids to audition if I'm doing it too."

Your smile couldn't get any wider if your face were made of rubber. "Have I mentioned lately how utterly awesome you are?"

Jessie blows on her fingernails and wipes them on her shirt. "Yeah, yeah. Tell me something I don't know."

As you move in to give Jessie a bear hug, Lena pipes up, "Well, I'll tell you something I do know—this is going to be an excellent angle for the blog! Two lifelong friends, united in justice, divided by competition . . . it's Pulitzer Prize–worthy!"

"Whoa, I wouldn't go that far," you protest. "Especially since we don't know who else is auditioning. We might both get blown out of the water!"

Lena pauses midtype. "Good point. Let's check out who else you're up against." Thank goodness, the crowd has thinned a little as kids have started heading back toward their homerooms. "Let's see," she says, scanning the list.

"Jasmine Viera, Lizette Tores, Kevin Minks, Megan Dunn . . . uh-oh . . ."

Note: It is never a good thing when one of your pals says "uh-oh."

"What's wrong?" Jessie asks. "Unless Taylor Swift herself is auditioning, I don't see a problem."

"You might want to look again," Lena answers, pointing toward the top of the list, where you see a name that fills you all with dread.

Mona Winston.

"Uh-oh," you and Jessie say at the same time.

You and Mona have had a rocky relationship ever since you stepped on her shoe when she first transferred to your school. You wish you could say you'd found a way to make peace with her since then, but the past few months have just made it worse. Mona and Jimmy were supposed to attend Shawna's *Charlie and the Chocolate Factory*–themed thirteenth birthday party together over the summer, but they had a big fight instead and haven't spoken much since. So the fact that everyone knows you and Jimmy have been hanging out a little hasn't exactly made Mona your biggest fan. (Not that she had ever been a fan of yours to begin with.)

"Oh, that's just perfect," you deadpan. "As if she doesn't hate me enough as it is, now she's going to see my signing up to audition as a personal challenge."

"But that's completely irrational," Lena reasons. "Half the school is auditioning."

"Yeah, but being rational isn't exactly what Mona is known for," you answer, that swirling feeling in your stomach getting stronger and stronger. "Could this get any worse?"

Wincing a little, Jessie sighs and says, "Well . . . yeah, it can." She slowly points out the list of kids who have signed up to be student judges.

Following her finger, you see that just as Amy predicted, Lisa Topple and Maria Santos are at the top of the list.

Great. So not only would you be going up against Mona—who usually gets what she wants—but also the judges' table will be chock-full of her entourage. Your Taylor Swift moment in New York is starting to look like more and more of a long shot.

You walk back to your homeroom dejectedly, making it inside just before the bell rings. As you grab your backpack and head toward your first class, you pass by the bulletin board again, where some kids have stopped to check out the lists. You are almost out of earshot when you hear Lisa squeal, "Ha! Is she serious? First she steals Mona's date, and now she's going to try and take her solo spot? That girl is deluded."

"No kidding," Maria answers. "She probably can't even sing. Mona is going to demolish her."

"Easily!" Lisa agrees.

With a chorus of giggles, they move on, while you are left frozen in the middle of the hallway. You have absolutely no doubt in your mind that they were just talking about you. But now you're full of doubts about yourself. You're not even sure you could speak right now, let alone sing. If only you could go somewhere to practice. . . . If Mona is as good as her fans seem to think, you definitely need some rehearsal time, pronto. Too bad you have history class next period. Or do you?

Brava! You were brave enough to throw your hat into the audition ring, even if the thought of actually going through with it does make you want to puke. Thank goodness for friends like Jessie, though. Who else would sign up for something so terrifying just so you won't have to go through it alone? But not everyone in the school is as fond of you as she is. Mona, who is most definitely not a fan of yours, is also going for a solo, and at least two of her friends will be sitting at the judges' table. As if that weren't enough, you overheard Lisa and Maria making snide comments about your chances, and you're not so sure they're wrong. Squeezing in some solid practice time could mean the difference between rock-star fame and hall of shame. But do you have it in you to cut class for the sake of your rep? The anticipation must be killing you. Take the quiz already!

QUIZ TIME!
Circle your answers and tally up the points at the end.

1. You are dying to see the new horror movie that just came out. It looks incredibly creepy and word has it some people have left the

theater in tears. Too bad it's rated R, which means no way you're getting to see it without an adult. What do you do?

A. Settle for seeing the new animated comedy. If you can't be scared to death, you can at least laugh your head off.

B. Beg your mom to take you to see it. Yes, you will probably have nightmares for a month, but you promise not to force her to sleep with every light on in the house—like you did the last time you saw a really scary movie.

C. Try to convince the ticket-booth person that you're of age. If the lipstick you swiped from your older sister's purse doesn't do the trick, maybe you can try making your voice a little deeper? Hey, it's worth a shot.

D. Buy a ticket for the animated movie, and then sneak into the horror flick. You know that's totally illegal, but keeping you from seeing the movie that everybody will be talking about is just ageism!

2. You've been invited to a friend's slumber party, but your folks won't let you go until your room—which is a total pigsty—is spotless. So you:

A. take your time and clean every nook and cranny. You will miss most of the festivities, but your room really does need a deep cleaning. And this way, you might not have to do this again for a while.

B. do a pretty good job, but stop short of dusting. You want your room clean, but let's not get crazy.

C. make your bed and then throw everything else in the

closet. With any luck, your parents won't think to check in there.

D. promise your little sister part of your allowance if she'll clean your room for you. Hey, your parents just said they wanted it clean. They didn't say *you* had to do it!

3. **Your best friend will be out of town for your birthday, so she's given you her gift early. But she made you promise not to open it until your actual bday. Do you stick to your word?**

A. Of course! When it comes to early presents, waiting is the rule.

B. You wait, but you call or text her every five minutes, asking questions to see if she'll drop any hints. You'll break her eventually.

C. Sort of. Shaking the box and holding it up to the light isn't against the rules, right?

D. No way! The second she's out of sight, you tear open the present, reasoning that if she really didn't want you to open it, she wouldn't have given it to you.

4. **Your crush asked you to go ice skating, just you and him, but your parents say you can't date until you're older. How do you handle it?**

A. You're bummed, but you respect their decision. You know they're just looking out for you. You and your crush can be good friends for now.

B. Invite him over for your grandparents' anniversary party instead. Maybe if your family gets to know him, they'll see what a great guy he is and will change their minds about the ice skating.

C. Hang out with him anyway, but only in group settings so that no one can tell you're actually on a date.

D. Tell your folks you're going to your best friend's house, but head for the skating rink. You even tell your friend to cover for you in case your parents call.

5. **There's a big test coming up in biology class that you are seriously unprepared for. What do you do?**

A. Study your brains out. Maybe if you work extra hard, you'll do all right.

B. Form a study group with some friends who you know take really careful notes. You may have slacked off a little, but it's never too late to benefit from someone else's hard work.

C. Take the test and just make some wild guesses. Lucky for you it's multiple choice. You're bound to get something right.

D. Try to get a peek at the teacher's edition of the textbook— the one with all the answers in it. Some might call that cheating. You call it efficient test taking.

Give yourself 1 point for every time you answered **A**, 2 points for every **B**, 3 points for every **C**, and 4 points for every **D**.

—If you scored between 5 and 12, go to page 68.

—If you scored between 13 and 20, go to page 56.

chapter
FOUR

The truth, the whole truth, and nothing but the truth: That's your motto. Your friends and family know that they can always depend on your honest opinion. And you never have to worry about getting caught up in lies, since they're just not your style. But while honesty is usually the best policy, make sure you're not being too blunt in the process. There's a difference between being up-front and being hurtful.

Jessie is eagerly awaiting your answer. She obviously thinks that her rendition of "You Belong with Me" was right on target. But the truth is she butchered it, and you're too good a friend to let her walk into that audition thinking anything else.

"Um," you begin hesitantly, "can I be honest?"

Jessie blinks in confusion. "Duh, of course you can! We're friends, aren't we?"

You sincerely hope she remembers that, once you tell her what you really think.

"Okay. Don't get mad, but your singing? Well, it needs a little work."

Jessie stares back at you blankly for a moment too long. "Are you kidding?"

"Sorry, but no. I'm being totally serious."

"Oh." The silence that follows is the very definition of awkward. She kind of shifts back and forth in her knee-high boots, looking everywhere but at your face. The faint freckles across the bridge of her nose have deepened to a darker brown, which tends to happen when she's blushing. You know you've embarrassed her by forcing her to sing and then basically telling her that she stinks. You won't be up for any friendship awards this year, you guess.

"Whatever," she says finally. "You're just saying that to be mean, because I have the guts to audition unlike *some* people I know."

Ouch. That hurt. Your hand flutters up to your chest as if Jessie has just punched you there. You can tell she immediately regrets saying that but is too hurt herself at the moment to apologize. This could easily turn into a silent-treatment war, but you don't want it to go that far. You know she's sorry, even if she can't say it. So you throw up your white flag first.

"Look, Jessie, you know I always tell you the truth. And I wouldn't have said anything if I weren't your friend. You get that, right?"

Jessie continues to stare at the floor, her head barely moving as she nods.

Encouraged, you keep going. "I think I can help you . . . if you'll let me." You stick your pinkie out to hook with hers. The pinkie shake is how you and your friends used to call a truce when you were in kindergarten. You remember friendship being a lot less complicated back then.

Jessie allows herself a grudging half smile. "Aw, now you've brought out the pinkies, so I guess I can't stay mad, can I?"

You break the tension with a ginormous (as Jessie would say) smile. "Nope! You sure can't. So how about we head back to homeroom before Ms. Campbell gives us detention? We can work on the song selection there."

"Sounds like a plan," Jessie says, reaching out her pinkie and giving yours a nice hard shake.

By the time the homeroom bell rings, you have figured out Jessie's problem. It isn't that she can't sing. It's just that the song you chose is way out of her range. Jessie is an alto, so she needs something in a lower register. Something like . . . Miley! Of course. Why didn't you think of that sooner?

As you and Jessie make your way toward history class, you quickly run through your iPod playlist, the two of you sharing your headphone earbuds. Thanks to Jessie, who still buys Miley CDs just so she can read the liner notes, you have a selection of her best songs at your fingertips. When you get to "7 Things" you know you've hit pay dirt.

"This is it!" you exclaim. "This one would be perfect for your voice." You pull Jessie over to a spot near the water fountains right before you get to class. "Why don't you try singing the chorus so I know for sure?"

She nervously hikes her JanSport backpack farther up on her shoulders, not making a peep. Wow, you never realized how easily her confidence could be shaken. She always seems so sure of herself. You guess you aren't the only one who sometimes feels like chickening out.

"Come on, Jess. Just trust me."

"All right, fine." She shrugs. "But if you laugh you're toast."

As soon as the first few bars leave her mouth, you realize you've struck gold. She sounds awesome! Nothing at all like what you heard during homeroom. You're about to tell her how incredible she is when someone else beats you to it.

"Oh my freaking God, Jessie, was that you singing just now? That was amazing!"

"Yeah, I totally thought Miley Cyrus was in the hallways for a second there."

Incredibly, these comments are coming from Lisa, Maria, and Shawna, three of the most popular girls in school. And you can tell by the sincere awe on their faces that they aren't being sarcastic at all. They're actually impressed.

"Oh wow, thanks!" Jessie yelps a little too loudly, clearly

caught off guard. "I'm, uh, well, I'm auditioning for a solo today, so I was just trying out my song."

Lisa, looking downtown chic with her bright red curls and tiny hoop earrings, offers her a delicate smile. "Well, they'd be fools not to give you a solo with a sound like that. You just have to come to lunch with us today. Can you?"

Maria, also very pretty (think Angelina Jolie as a thirteen-year-old), nods her head. "Definitely. You have to come. We won't take no for an answer."

The girls are pointedly looking directly into Jessie's eyes and ignoring you completely (their way of making it very clear that they are talking to Jess, not you). Your shock at hearing them suddenly invite Jessie to lunch, after years of barely acknowledging her existence, only intensifies when Jessie quickly says, "Sure! See you in the caf!"

Okay, is there a full moon outside? Has the whole planet shifted on its axis? Something must be up, because never have these girls invited Jessie to sit with them at lunch. Well, not since second grade anyway (pre-cliques). You've always thought of Jessie as all that and a bag of chips, but for them to think it now is just . . . weird.

"Cool, see ya later, then," Shawna says smoothly as she and the other girls head off to their own class. She at least waves to you quickly.

You turn back to Jessie, expecting her to be all *What the heck?* after her earlier rant about taking down the popular kids. But to your surprise, Jessie can hardly keep her eyes in her head, and she's having trouble closing her mouth.

"Did that just happen?" she asks. "How cool!" Without waiting for you, she heads into history class sporting a whole new strut.

Hmm. Guess even Jessie is not immune to the lure of the popular clique. She seems not to have noticed that you weren't really part of that little lovefest. To answer her question, yes, that did just happen. You saw it with your own two eyes. You're just not sure *why* it happened.

Thank goodness you and Jessie are close enough friends that you can tell each other the truth and survive. She was mad at you at first for dissing her singing ability, but thankfully, she came around and let you help her. And now she sounds amazing! Everything seems to be looking up until Lisa and Maria come out of nowhere and throw you for a loop. Since when have they invited Jessie into their inner sanctum? You'd like to think their motives are pure, but you're just not sure what to believe. Do you take their actions at face value, or do you smell a rat? Maybe you'll be less confused after the quiz.

QUIZ TIME!

Circle your answers and tally up the points at the end.

1. You get an e-mail that says if you forward it to twenty people, you'll have good luck for seven years. If you don't, you'll have bad luck for life. Do you forward the e-mail?

A. Totally! The world is tough enough as it is. You really don't want to bring on a guaranteed lifetime of bad luck.

B. Sure. You only forward it to your closest friends, though. You don't want any bad luck, but who has time to send an e-mail chain to twenty people?

C. Well, you forward it to your best friend just in case. But you're not too worried. It probably won't affect you at all. You hope.

D. No way. You don't believe that forwarding e-mails can bring you good luck. As a matter of fact, you're a firm believer in making your own luck.

2. **A girl at school who has always been awful to you gives you a heads-up that there's going to be a pop quiz in math today. She even offers you her notes. You react by:**

A. thanking her and inviting her to your lunch table so that you can study together. Maybe she's not so bad after all.

B. thanking her and gratefully taking her notes. You're not sure why she's being so nice, but maybe she's had a change of heart.

C. thanking her for the info but telling her you'll use your own notes. If she's telling the truth, you appreciate the warning. But what if her notes are full of wrong answers and she's trying to set you up?

D. refusing her notes in case she's feeding you wrong answers, then immediately asking around to see if anyone else has heard about a quiz. Most likely she just lied to see if you would panic.

3. Your favorite tabloid has a great section that lists all the new gossip–who's dating who, who's feuding with who–you know, the good stuff. How much of it do you believe?

A. All of it! The celebs might try to deny the stories, but the mags wouldn't print them if they weren't true, right?

B. Almost all of it. The part about your two favorite singers being nuts was probably blown out of proportion, but you wholeheartedly buy the rest.

C. Most of it. The cast members of that new show are definitely dating one another. But the celebrity feuds rundown was probably made up to boost sales.

D. You don't believe any of that mumbo jumbo. Everybody knows the tabloids can't be trusted. But they sure are fun to read!

4. You're the leader for a group project in school. Johnny, a notorious slacker, is in your group. He has a major role in the presentation and promises to pull his weight. So you:

A. trust him completely. If he says he'll come through, then you're sure he will. You're glad to be able to relax and focus on your own share of the work.

B. believe him, but check in on his progress every few days just to make sure.

C. let him handle his part, but secretly prepare his section on your own, just in case he slips back into his lazy ways. You know he has the best intentions, but he doesn't have the best track record.

D. assign him a less important role in the project—like

announcing your group name or something. No way are you leaving your grade in Johnny's hands. You doubt he'll deliver.

5. **A new sneaker just came out that promises to make you run faster, jump higher, and be cooler. Do you buy them?**

   A. Of course! You're sure that as soon as you lace those puppies up, you'll be able to run a mile a minute!

   B. Yes. Even if they don't make you jump any higher, they're bound to score you some cool points at school.

   C. Maybe. You don't really think they'll help your softball game at all, but if there's even the slightest chance that they will, you'll give them a shot.

   D. Nah. No sneaker can make you run faster. Those ads always exaggerate the truth.

*Give yourself 1 point for every time you answered **A**, 2 points for every **B**, 3 points for every **C**, and 4 points for every **D**.*

—If you scored between 5 and 12, go to page 89.

—If you scored between 13 and 20, go to page 76.

chapter FIVE

Liar, liar, pants on fire. It's understandable that once in a while you tell little white lies to avoid hurting someone's feelings. (Who doesn't?) But sometimes you tell some whoppers that make it hard for people to trust you. Don't allow insecurity, boredom, or fear of not being liked to rule you, ultimately forcing you to mask who you are. The real you is worth knowing—as are your real opinions.

Jessie is staring at you expectantly, waiting for your response. You should tell her she's awful, terrible, really bad. You should tell her you've heard car alarms that sound better than she does. But what comes out is:

"Wow! That was really . . . great!" You shout it out with

a hollow clap, hoping she won't notice that you're cringing inside.

She claps along in glee. "You really think so?"

Here's yet another chance to tell her the truth. Come on, you can do it.

"Most def. You're going to be a star!"

Okay, maybe we should have established the definition of "truth" first. You do own a dictionary, right?

"I knew it!" Jessie yells, jumping up and down. "I won't let you down!" She swoops back into homeroom, floating on air, while you follow her in feeling like you're sinking in quicksand. You really want to be honest with Jess, but you just don't have the heart. How do you tell someone they aren't soloist material without wrecking their confidence? More important, how do you tell one of your best friends in the whole world that her singing stinks without making her hate you forever?

There has to be a better way. And after the bell rings, cueing the change of classes, you think maybe you've found it. As you walk by the bulletin board again, spying Jessie's fancy signature on the solo sheet, your eyes drift over to the sheet next to it, the one for student judges.

Already it is reading like a who's who of popular kids. Lisa Topple, Maria Santos, Shawna Levin, Steven Oh, Adam Arap, Adam Arap, Adam Arap . . .

No, there aren't three Adams signed up. You're just reading the name over and over again because you secretly think he is pretty cute. At first glance, Adam seems like a total preppy, with his khaki pants, blue polo shirt, and neat, silky blond hair that falls in a swoop over his left eye. But something about his tendency to never say more than a few words at a time, and his habit of tapping his fingers against things as if he's playing the drums, gives him a sort of rock-musician swagger. Maybe it's just the fact that when he smiles he reminds you of Kris Allen, one of the most adorable *American Idol* winners in the show's history. If you weren't already crushing on Jimmy Morehouse, Adam would definitely be next in line. As for the other people on the list, you've always reluctantly admired them (they're the closest thing your school has to celebrities, after all), but other than borrowing the occasional pencil, you never really have an excuse to talk to them. Even though you were all friends in second grade, somewhere along the way they became part of one camp and you became part of another, and up until now it seemed like it would always be that way.

But that's not why you find yourself grabbing the pen next to the sheet and signing your name under Adam's. You do it because it hits you that signing up as a judge is the only way Jessie will have a fighting chance at the auditions. Even if no one else votes for her, you will, so at least she won't be completely shut out. It's a brilliant plan, one more thing you're willing to do for the cause. Getting to sit next to Adam at the judges' table will merely be a perk, a little reward for your selflessness.

You're about to head off to class when Shawna Levin and

Dionne Williams come by to check out the lists. "Hey," Shawna says, "you're going to be a student judge too?"

You shrug shyly. "I guess so." Shawna was only sort of popular last year. But after she threw the birthday party of the century over the summer, she reached legendary status.

"Cool," Dionne says. "I'm glad I'm not the only jock signing up to judge instead of sing. Can you believe Mark is going for it? Would someone tell that kid he can't sing already?"

You laugh in relief. They aren't planning to make fun of you for thinking you can infiltrate their clique—they're actually including you.

"I know, right?" you say. "Wait, you think I'm a jock?"

Dionne and Shawna look at each other in momentary confusion. "Well, yeah," Dionne answers. "You *are* the MVP on the girls' soccer team, aren't you?"

Oh yeah. Of course you are. But you had never thought of yourself as part of the "jock" clique because of it. You just play because you love it. But maybe you haven't been as off the popular kids' radar as you thought.

"Yep, that's me!" you exclaim proudly. "Somebody's gotta make the goals around here."

Dionne laughs. "Finally! Someone who understands. See, Shawna? It's not that I *want* to be the star server on the volleyball team. It's just that somebody has to step up, so it might as well be me." She pats her microbraids, batting her eyelashes furiously.

"Yeah, yeah, yeah," Shawna answers. "You're a regular Gabrielle Reece."

You are clearly overhearing a conversation that the two of them have all the time. Kind of the way you and Jessie always give Lena grief over her obsession with Shakespeare. You're being included in their private joke, and you have to admit it feels pretty good.

So good, in fact, that when you reach the end of the hallway, you're a little disappointed to find they are turning left and you're heading right.

"We'll see you around, okay?" Shawna calls as they walk off.

"Yeah, us student judges have to stick together!" Dionne adds, holding up a peace sign.

You flash one back, and for the first time in who knows how long, you feel . . . cool.

After your next class, you text Lena to let her know that you signed up to be a student judge—although you don't tell her you did it because Jessie is a terrible singer. (As far as she knows, it's all part of the plan.) You also leave out the brief but meaningful exchange you had with Shawna and Dionne. You're not sure why. Maybe you think Lena would be jealous, or that she'd be suspicious of your new friends. But it could also be because this morning you vowed to bring down all the powerful cliques in the school. And now that you're sorta kinda friends with Shawna and

Dionne, you don't exactly want to anymore. Not now, when you might actually have a chance at being at the top of the totem pole for once.

You really hate to admit this, but maybe your signing up to be a student judge didn't have anything to do with Jessie at all. Maybe you just wanted to be part of that in-crowd. You are still trying to figure yourself out as you enter the cafeteria for lunch. Perhaps you should have thought this whole thing through a little more before you walked head on into a social war zone.

After you get your tray of food (cold pizza, green beans, and chocolate milk), you look up to find two groups of people waving you over to join them. On one side is your usual crew: Jessie, Lena, Charlie, Lizette, and Jimmy—who is looking adorable as ever with little splotches of red paint in his dark hair. He's wearing a beat-up plaid button-down over a plain white T-shirt, which makes his deep green eyes look even greener.

Usually it would be a no-brainer to go sit with them. But on the other side of the cafeteria, in front of the windows, you see Shawna and Dionne, who have saved you a seat across from the unnaturally cute Adam Arap. Next to Adam are Maria and Lisa. And suddenly it dawns on you why you are being invited over: They are student judges, so you actually have a good reason to join them. Maybe they want to talk about official judge stuff and it's very, very important.

All right, even Lena's cat wouldn't buy that one. If you do

sit by the windows, it won't be because you think you have some duty to your fellow judges. It'll be because you are really tempted to spend some time over on Planet Popular. Who wouldn't be?

Aside from Jessie, Lena, Charlie, Lizette, and Jimmy, that is.

Where is a good clone when you need one? You feel like you've been put in one awkward position after another today. You managed to get out of auditioning, only to find yourself having to lie to one of your best friends in the world. And now you're being torn between two cafeteria tables. You don't want to diss your buds, but you also don't wanna miss out on a chance to be superpopular, if only for one lunch period. It's the ultimate social dilemma: Do you stick with the true-blue team you've got—or do you take a shot at the big leagues? Still haven't decided? Let the quiz choose for you.

QUIZ TIME!

Circle your answers and tally up the points at the end.

1. You've been invited to two parties on the same night. One is being hosted by Cheyenne, your slightly nerdy but very sweet pal from summer camp. The other is being thrown by Jodi, the cool girl you just met in English class. Your plan is to:

    A. go to Cheyenne's party, of course. You feel bad saying no to Jodi, but Cheyenne asked you first. There won't be many people there, and it'll probably be pretty low-key (we're talking Monopoly and a *Vampire Diaries* marathon), but Cheyenne is a good friend, and that's all you need to have fun.

B. go to Cheyenne's party but leave early so that you can make an appearance at Jodi's place. Cheyenne is great, but you don't want Jodi to think you would say no if she invited you to her next throwdown.

C. head to Jodi's party, dance up a storm, then take off and show up at Cheyenne's for ice cream. By the time you get there, you'll have missed all the board games and Netflix videos, but you're sure Cheyenne will understand.

D. skip Cheyenne's place and party it up at Jodi's house. Your summer camp buddy is nice and all, but getting in good with Jodi could be the key to your entire social life!

2. **It is your first week in a new school and you have a ton of activities to choose from. Whatever you go with will set the tone for your whole school year. You pick:**

A. the book club. It isn't the most social of clubs (you'll be spending most of your time as a member reading alone in your room), but you love books and you'd choose a really good novel over a really good party any day.

B. the chess club. Sure, chess might attract a slightly nerdier crowd (which means your name won't exactly be the first one on the guest list when it comes to the cool parties), but you think chess can be exciting! Competing against just one other person to see who can outsmart who, who can think several moves ahead to end up with a checkmate . . . bring it on!

C. student government. You'll be involved in making decisions for the whole school, so you'll meet a ton of people. (Of course, you'll have to make some tough choices that some kids might not like, which means they might not like you.)

D. cheerleading. The most popular girls are on the squad, and you'll get to go to all the football games. Not to mention you'll get to wear a uniform, so the whole school will know you're part of an elite group. Definitely where you need to be.

3. **Several weeks ago your best guy friend asked you to go to the spring dance with him and you agreed. But a few days before the dance, Mark, the cutest guy in school, asks you too. What do you do?**

A. Stick with your original date. He asked you first, and you would never back out on a friend. The two of you will have a ton of fun together.

B. Tell Mark you can't go with him since you already agreed to go with someone else, but promise to save him a dance.

C. Stay with your date . . . at least until you get to the dance. Then sneak away to spend most of your time with Mr. Popular. You're sure your friend will understand. It isn't every day that a guy like Mark looks your way.

D. Break the news to your friend that you got a better offer and go to the dance with Mark. Yes, your original date might be mad at first, but he'll get over it. He wouldn't want you to pass up a great opportunity like that, right?

4. **When you grow up, you hope to have a career as:**
   A. a veterinarian. You'll be surrounded by animals every day and get to save tons of furry creatures.
   B. a travel writer. You'll spend lots of time alone writing, but you'll also get to travel to exotic places and meet the locals.
   C. an event planner. You're a social butterfly, so by planning events, you'll always be at the center of all the action.
   D. a VJ on MTV. You'll interview all the hottest celebrities and get invited to the coolest parties. Diddy could use a new partner in crime. That could be you!

5. **This year's school musical is a production of _Grease_. What part do you go for?**
   A. The stage crew. It's not glamorous, but you'd much rather be behind the scenes than in the spotlight.
   B. Part of the chorus. You won't stand out much, but you'll get to appear onstage and your name will be in the play-bill. That's good enough for you!
   C. One of the Pink Ladies—maybe Frenchy. You don't have that many lines, but the ones you do have are memorable. Plus, you'll get to hang out with all the leads.

D. Sandy, of course! She is the star of the show. If you get that part, everyone will know your name.

Give yourself 1 point for every time you chose *A*, 2 points for every *B*, 3 points for every *C*, and 4 points for every *D*.

—If you scored between 5 and 12, go to page 112.

—If you scored between 13 and 20, go to page 99.

chapter
SIX

Rules were made to be broken, as far as you're concerned. Most of them don't make sense anyway, so whenever possible you try to find a way around them. Some might call you a troublemaker, but you'd prefer to think of yourself as a rebel. What you seem to be missing, though, is that some of the rules you're rebelling against were made for a reason. Must you learn everything the hard way?

Not that you make a habit of this, but instead of heading to history class, you veer off course and head downstairs toward the art room. You know that it's always empty during this period. And you also happen to know that the room has great acoustics, so you can practice your little heart out.

Speaking of hearts, yours is beating a mile a minute as you sneak into the quiet room and close the door behind you. You're pretty sure no one saw you come in. With any luck, your history teacher won't even notice you're not in class. What's important now is that you have time to warm up your pipes.

After you put your backpack down on an empty desk, you try to calm your runaway heart with a few deep breaths, taking in the faint smell of acrylic paint. Then, just as you learned to do in music class last year, you run through a few scales, letting your voice rise and fall: "me, meee, Meee, MEEEE, Meee, meee, me." Finally, you face the row of easels and big blank canvases, pretending they are the audience for the choir auditions.

Even though you know the easels are not real people, you're suddenly nervous all the same. You feel your palms get clammy as you launch into the first few bars of "You Belong with Me." As you run through the song, you make a mental note not to shake any of the judges' hands. The last thing you want them to remember you as is Ms. Sweaty Palms.

You finish up your first run-through of the Taylor Swift tune, picturing the judges going wild, clapping till their hands are sore. But wait . . . is your imagination that good, or is that real clapping you hear? It seems to be coming from behind the large canvas on an easel in the back of the room.

"Um . . . is anybody there?" you venture, hoping the answer is yes. Otherwise, you might be losing your marbles a little bit.

Slowly the clapping stops and someone pokes his head out from behind the canvas. When you see who it is, your heart nearly gallops out of your chest.

Jimmy Morehouse—your friend and ongoing megacrush.

"Oh my God," you mutter. "Have you been here the whole time?"

He nods shyly, his messy black hair perfectly complementing his plain white T-shirt and ratty-looking flannel button-down. You can feel all the blood in your body rush to your face. Jimmy is in your history class—which is why you never expected him to be working in the art room right now. If it's possible to die of embarrassment, it might happen right now.

You shove your hands into the back pockets of your jeans to stop them from shaking. "Sorry you had to hear that," you tell Jimmy. "It was probably terrible. Hope it didn't kill your creativity or anything."

Jimmy looks at you with sincere green eyes, shaking his head. "Terrible? Are you kidding? That was . . . Wow. You can really sing. I didn't know."

You notice a look of honest admiration register on his face as he stares at you, his lips parted slightly and his eyebrows raised in surprise.

"Really?" you ask. You're not fishing for compliments. You just want to make sure you're not caught up in some superrealistic daydream.

"Really," Jimmy confirms, smiling.

You smile back, your heart finally easing up its pace. "Thanks," you say. "But, um, what are you doing in here anyway? Are you cutting history class too?" Is it possible Jimmy is as much of a rebel as you are?

"Who, me?" Jimmy answers, pointing to himself. "Nah. I got permission from the principal to spend some extra time working on my pieces for the art show this afternoon."

Oh yeah! You've been so caught up in the choir madness that you almost forgot about Jimmy's big art debut.

"Jeez, that's right!" you exclaim, slowly walking toward Jimmy and sitting on a stool next to him—right after he throws a cloth over his canvas so that you can't see what he was working on. "Today's the big day for you. You must be so excited!"

Jimmy shrugs. "I guess. But . . . can I tell you a secret?"

"Sure," you answer, flattered that he would choose you to confide in.

"Well, uh, the truth is, I'm terrified." He laughs nervously. "This is embarrassing, but when I agreed to be part of the exhibit, it didn't occur to me that I'd have to show my work to everybody!"

You laugh a little, feeling yourself relax. How great is it to know that you aren't the only one walking around scared out of your mind? "Yeah, that's the thing about the word 'exhibit.' It usually involves exhibiting stuff."

"Real funny," Jimmy answers flatly. "You probably think I'm king of the dorks now, huh?"

"Hey!" you object. "Not true at all! I thought that *way* before now." You gently bump his shoulder with your own and give him a big smile to show him you're kidding. No way could you ever think of Jimmy as a dork.

"If it makes you feel any better," you continue, "the reason I'm here right now is because I'm terrified too. Like an idiot, I signed up to audition for a choir solo today, and now I have to compete against Mona!"

Jimmy winces. Since he spent a little time with Mona over the summer, he knows how scary she can be, and that she doesn't like anyone coming between her and something she wants. "Yeah, I can see how that would throw you off," he says seriously. "But look, you have nothing to worry about. From what I just heard, you've got this choir thing in the bag."

"Thanks, Jimmy. And you shouldn't worry about the art show. You're really, really good. Everyone's going to flip when they see what you can do."

He smiles gratefully and takes a deep breath. "I hope so. But how about we do something fun to get our minds off all this pressure?" He hands you a paintbrush and reaches for a small spare canvas.

For the next few minutes, Jimmy gives you an art lesson, teaching you how to paint someone's portrait using each other as models. He shows you how to use the color wheel to mix paint colors and how to get the proportions right, then he leaves you on your own. A few minutes later you are ready to reveal your masterpiece.

"Voilà!" you cry in a horrible French accent. "It eez a work of art."

Jimmy comes to stand behind you and view your painting. "Well, it's a work of something," he says doubtfully. Okay, you're not exactly van Gogh. You have painted Jimmy as a stick figure with a nest of black hair and two globs of green paint for eyes. And even though his arms and legs are just sticks, they're crooked, and his legs are about a mile long. You both end up laughing hysterically.

"And what are those?" Jimmy says through tears of laughter, reaching over your shoulder to point at what looks like two bolts.

"Um, I think those are your ears."

"On my neck?" Jimmy manages to say before doubling over in laughter again.

You can't even remember the last time you laughed this hard. You still have the jitters about the audition (or maybe you're shaking because you're standing so close to Jimmy?), but this art thing is fun . . . not to mention kind of romantic.

"Here, let me show you where the ears should go, Picasso," Jimmy says, his fingers brushing against yours as he reaches for the paintbrush in your hand.

But just then, the door swings open and the art teacher,

Ms. Darbeau, sweeps into the room. As soon as she sees you, she folds her arms and her lips harden into a tight line. "Well, well, well . . . ," she says. "I suppose I should be happy that you're finally discovering art, young lady. But I know that you are *not* supposed to be in my art room right now. Which means you must be cutting class—perhaps to pursue other *interests*." On that last word she raises an eyebrow at Jimmy.

Oh man, you are *so* busted.

On your way to the principal's office, Ms. Darbeau informs you that cutting class is a serious offense. Jimmy isn't in trouble since he had permission to be there, but you have no excuse.

"I must admit, I'm surprised," Principal Kern says as he folds his hands in front of him on the desk. "According to your schedule, you were supposed to be in history class. And your teacher verified that you didn't show up at all today. It isn't like you to cut class to flirt with a boy. . . ."

You're sure your face just turned ten shades of red. "That isn't what I—I mean, that's not why I cut class."

"Oh no?" the principal says. "Then what was it?"

You stare miserably at your worn-out sneakers. "I wanted to practice my song for the choir audition."

Hearing it out loud, you know it doesn't sound like a very good reason.

Principal Kern sighs. "In that case, I won't send you to detention."

"You won't?" you ask hopefully. Is it possible you're about to get off scot-free thanks to your talent? Could it be that Principal Kern believes in your dream?

"No, I won't," he answers. "In light of the fact that you broke the rules and cut class in order to sing, I think a much more fitting consequence would be to ban you from the auditions."

NOOOOOO!!!!!

As you walk dejectedly to your next class, you sulk over ruining your chance at stardom. You might as well call Jessie to let her know that the mission to upset the social order is all up to her now. After you hit her speed-dial button, Jessie picks up quickly, and you break the horrible news.

You expect her to be upset, or at least nervous, but instead she sounds downright chipper.

"Aw, that's okay, really," Jessie chirps.

"It is?" you ask, not quite believing her. "You have to audition solo now. I thought you'd be mad."

"Well, I might have been, but Lisa and Maria saw that I put my name on the sign-up sheet, and their whole posse has been sooo nice to me ever since. Can you believe it? They even offered to help me with my audition!"

Okay, everything about that last sentence sounds wrong, wrong, wrong. Since when have those girls wanted to help Jessie with anything? And why would they want to start now, when their queen bee, Mona, is also up for the soloist spot? Something seems mighty fishy.

Well, this is a most unfortunate turn of events. You got busted skipping class and as a result, your audition dreams are donezo. Getting in some quality flirting time with Jimmy was almost worth the sacrifice. But now the crushing of the cliques is all up to Jessie. And judging by the last phone call you had with her, it doesn't sound like she's your best bet anymore. The popular girls seem to have convinced her that she's one of them now. If they really do want to help her, that's great. But you have a feeling there's more to their sudden friendship than meets the eye. Are you onto something, or is the skeptic in you just being paranoid? Let's see what the quiz has to say.

QUIZ TIME!

Circle your answers and tally up the points at the end.

1. You get an e-mail that says if you forward it to twenty people, you'll have good luck for seven years. If you don't, you'll have bad luck for life. Do you forward the e-mail?

    A. Totally! The world is tough enough as it is. You really don't want to bring on a guaranteed lifetime of bad luck.

    B. Sure. You only forward it to your closest friends, though. You don't want any bad luck, but who has time to send an e-mail chain to twenty people?

    C. Well, you forward it to your best friend just in case. But you're not too worried. It probably won't affect you at all. You hope.

D. No way. You don't believe that forwarding e-mails can bring you good luck. As a matter of fact, you're a firm believer in making your own luck.

2. **A girl you don't get along with at school gives you a heads-up that there's going to be a pop quiz in math today. She even offers you her notes. You react by:**

A. thanking her and inviting her to your lunch table so that you can study together. Maybe she's not so bad after all.

B. thanking her and gratefully taking her notes. You're not sure why she's being so nice, but maybe she's had a change of heart.

C. thanking her for the info but telling her you'll use your own notes. If she's telling the truth, you appreciate the warning. But what if her notes are full of wrong answers and she's trying to set you up?

D. refusing her notes in case she's feeding you wrong answers, then immediately asking around to see if anyone else has heard about a quiz. Most likely she just lied to see if you would panic.

3. **Your favorite tabloid has a great section that lists all the new gossip—who's dating who, who's feuding with who—you know, the good stuff. How much of it do you believe?**

A. All of it! The celebs might try to deny the stories, but the mags wouldn't print them if they weren't true, right?

B. Almost all of it. The part about your two favorite singers being nuts was probably blown out of proportion, but you wholeheartedly buy the rest.

C. Most of it. The cast members of that new show are definitely dating one another. But the celebrity feuds rundown was probably made up to boost sales.

D. You don't believe any of that mumbo jumbo. Everybody knows the tabloids can't be trusted. But they sure are fun to read!

4. **You're the leader for a group project in school. Johnny, a notorious slacker, is in your group. He has a major role in the presentation and promises to pull his weight. So you:**

A. trust him completely. If he says he'll come through, then you're sure he will. You're glad to be able to relax and focus on your own share of the work.

B. believe him, but check in on his progress every few days just to make sure.

C. let him handle his part but secretly prepare his section on your own, just in case he slips back into his lazy ways. You know he has the best intentions, but he doesn't have the best track record.

D. assign him a less important role in the project—like announcing your group name or something. No way are you leaving your grade in Johnny's hands. You doubt he'll deliver.

5. **A new sneaker just came out that promises to make you run faster, jump higher, and be cooler. Do you buy them?**

   A. Of course! You're sure that as soon as you lace those puppies up, you'll be able to run a mile a minute!

   B. Yes. Even if they don't make you jump any higher, they'll definitely score you some cool points at school.

   C. Maybe. You don't really think they'll help your softball game at all, but if there is even the slightest chance that they will, you'll give them a shot.

   D. Nah. No sneaker can make you run faster. Those ads always exaggerate the truth.

Give yourself 1 point for every time you answered *A*, 2 points for every *B*, 3 points for every *C*, and 4 points for every *D*.

   —If you scored between 5 and 12, go to page 89.

   —If you scored between 13 and 20, go to page 76.

chapter
SEVEN

You're a rules girl. You tend to do things by the book and very rarely get in trouble because of that. At a time when some of your friends are rebelling against everything, you rebel against rebellion. It's not that you're crazy about all the rules you have to live by. But you respect them (as long as they're fair) and know that you'll get to make your own someday.

As much as you would love to get in some practice before the audition, you head to history class as scheduled. If you do score a solo spot, you don't want it to be because you cut class. (Detention would probably be the least of your worries if that happened.)

Too bad the only reward you get for your good behavior is seeing Mona's snarling face as soon as you walk through the door. You know for sure that life is unfair, because if it weren't, you wouldn't have any classes with Mona. She's lucky it isn't true that if you make an ugly face for too long, it stays that way, because her modeling career would have been over a long time ago.

You take your seat and do your best to ignore her glares, focusing instead on Ms. Krell's lesson for the day: Napoleon's quest for power. You are furiously taking notes about the events leading up to Waterloo when you feel your bag vibrate at your feet. It's your cell phone, letting you know you have a text message. You aren't supposed to text in class, but curiosity gets the best of you.

Without drawing too much attention to yourself, you reach into your bag and pull out your phone, flipping it open under your desk. You click on the little envelope icon and get the nastiest shock of your morning so far. Mona has sent you a text message:

> U don't stand a chance against
> me in choir. Drop out now!

You close the phone and try to keep your face stone still, as if you'd just read another perfectly normal text from Lena or Jessie. You refuse to give Mona the satisfaction of getting a rise out of you! Instead you'll concentrate on how Napoleon conquered so much of his empire.

But as you're scribbling away in your notebook, your phone vibrates again.

> U probly don't even know what
> 2 sing l8tr. What a joke.

That's it. You tried to take the high road, but you can't bear it anymore. Who does she think she is anyway? You flip open the keyboard on your phone and furiously type back a message.

> I'll B singing U B long with Me
> and it's going to rock!!!

There! That ought to shut her up. Of course, just as you're hitting Send you see a shadow loom over your desk.

"Care to share what you're writing with the whole class?" Ms. Krell asks you. "I mean, whatever it is must be awfully important, since you know good and well texting is not allowed in my classroom."

Sigh. You do have a choice here. You could tell Ms. Krell that Mona started it by texting you first. But what are you, in kindergarten? Besides, one thing you aren't is a snitch. Telling on Mona probably won't get you out of hot water anyway. So you figure the safest thing to do is say nothing and try your best to melt into your chair.

"Hand it over," Ms. Krell demands, holding out her hand. You were afraid of that. Ms. Krell's greatest joy in life is confiscating what she considers contraband in her classroom: Cell phones, PSPs, gum, iPods, magazines . . . the list is endless. But cell phones are definitely at the top of her hit list of classroom no-nos.

You plop the phone into her hand, praying that will be the end of it. But noooo. . . .

"I'll be holding on to this phone until tomorrow."

Your mouth gapes open. Tomorrow? That's practically a lifetime away. You've heard of living off the grid, but this is ridiculous. And she isn't even finished yet.

"Since you seem bored and want to do something with your hands, maybe you'll enjoy spending your lunch period cleaning up the library. As you know, it's in quite a state. But with nimble fingers like yours"—she wiggles your phone in the air—"you should be done in no time." With that, she turns with military precision back toward the chalkboard and continues rattling off facts about Napoleon.

You don't even need to look over at Mona to know that she's smiling from ear to ear. Ugh. The scoreboard so far: Mona—1, you—big fat goose egg.

You have always been a good girl, a law-abiding citizen, someone who plays by the rules. So why did you end up in trouble? Even though you were tempted to skip class, you went to history like you were supposed to, only to get baited into a text-message war by none other than Mona

Winston. Without even breaking a sweat, she managed to get you riled up, your cell phone confiscated, and your precious freedom taken away. Okay, maybe the last one is overstating it a bit, but you will be missing out on lunch with your friends (one of your favorite pastimes) in order to clean up the disaster area that is the school library. You might as well be heading off to jail. Your only hope of saving face is to finish cleaning early so that you have time to plead your way back into your teacher's good graces and reclaim your phone. But come on, is it even possible to clean such a massive mess before lunch is over? Take the quiz to find out if you have the drive to get the job done.

QUIZ TIME!
Circle your answers and tally up the points at the end.

1. **You really, really, really want the new iPhone, but your folks won't spring for it. They think you should get a job this summer to save up the money. What job do you go for?**

   A. A paper route in your neighborhood. You'll have to wake up at the crack of dawn every morning and it will be hard work, but it pays well, you'll get some exercise, and you'll have your iPhone in no time.

   B. You apply to help out at the local pool. You'll have to help clean the locker rooms, but you'll also get to swim and lie out by the pool during slow times.

   C. Apply to take tickets at the nearby movie theater. You'll barely have to do anything and you'll even get to see some movies. It doesn't pay that much, but at least you won't have to break a sweat.

D. Get a job? Hellloooo, it's called summer vacation for a reason. No way are you going to ruin two straight months of freedom just to get an iPhone. You don't want one that badly anyway.

2. **You have to present a research paper in English class. It counts for a lot of your grade, so the teacher gives you lots of time to prepare. Naturally, you:**

A. write a really well-researched paper, adding a few more pages than you needed. Plus you throw in a PowerPoint presentation and handouts. You're after an A⁺ so you go all out.

B. write a paper that is exactly what the teacher asked for, no more, no less. The teacher thinks you could have done better, but come on, you do have a life.

C. hand in a paper that is a little shorter than the teacher asked for. But for something you just threw together over the weekend, it isn't bad. It won't get you anywhere near an A, but it'll keep you out of summer school!

D. try to use a paper you wrote for last semester's English class. Sure, you could have written a five-star paper if you'd wanted to, but who actually wants to do that much work?

3. **You have a snow day off from school. What do you do with it?**

A. Catch up on all your school assignments, reorganize your closet, update your blog, squeeze in a workout, and read a few chapters of the great book you just bought.

B. Get a few chores out of the way so you have more of your weekend free. Then spend some quality time with your little sis. (You did promise to help her decorate her dollhouse a while ago.)

C. Go have a snowball fight with some friends, and then get warm again by drinking some hot cocoa and playing board games with your family.

D. Sleep till noon, and then spend the rest of the day in your pj's vegging in front of the TV. That's what snow days are for!

4. **You and some friends join the talent show planning committee. The faculty advisor asks for volunteers for various roles. What do you volunteer to do?**

A. Head up the whole committee. If you want the show to come out right, you'll have to step up to the plate.

B. Be in charge of the music. That way you'll have to worry about only one aspect of the show.

C. The least taxing job possible, like posting the talent show announcement on the school's Web site. The less you have to do, the better.

D. Before you get sucked into taking on too much, you ease your way off the committee. You have enough on your plate as it is, and taking on extra stuff will seriously cut into your free time.

5. **You're babysitting your neighbor's kids for a few hours, and they're bored—and driving you crazy. What do you do to pass the time?**

A. Write a short play for the kids to perform for their parents, complete with costumes and props. What kid wouldn't love that? And being so busy makes the hours fly by.

B. Play hide-and-seek. They always hide in the same places, but you take extra long to find them anyway just to savor the peace and quiet.

C. Give them a stack of paper and a giant box of crayons and let them go wild. You get to supervise from the couch.

D. Sit them in front of the TV watching cartoons while you gab on the phone with your friends. This babysitting business is a piece of cake!

Give yourself 1 point for every time you answered **A**, 2 points for every **B**, 3 points for every **C**, and 4 points for every **D**.

—If you scored between 5 and 12, go to page 135.

—If you scored between 13 and 20, go to page 123.

chapter
EIGHT

good for you! Because you're such a skeptical chick, no one is going to put anything over on you. You don't believe everything you see on TV, in magazines, or on the Internet. And you take what other people tell you with a grain of salt—especially if you've been burned by them in the past. That means your critical thinking skills are in good working order. However, not believing anything can be just as bad as believing everything. It's great that you are by no means gullible, but the ability to give people the benefit of the doubt could allow them to surprise you—in a good way.

You feel like you must have accidentally stepped into another dimension and ended up in bizarro land. That is the only plausible explanation for Lisa and Maria suddenly accepting Jessie into their exclusive inner circle. Not that Jessie isn't totally A-list in your book, but those girls usually treat anyone who isn't a part of their posse like they're strictly D-list. So, why the sudden change?

Yes, the song you had Jessie sing did make her sound light-years better than she did before. But you don't buy that Lisa was just bowled over by Jessie's vocal stylings. Something is definitely going on. And if you had to guess, you'd say that whatever it is, you wouldn't like it.

In light of that fact, you don't feel the least bit bad about channeling your inner Nancy Drew and following Lisa and Maria between classes to see what they're up to. As they make their way down the stairs and past the library, you start to get a little nervous. They are heading straight for the cluster of lockers outside the auditorium, where there isn't too much traffic, which means there won't be anywhere for you to hide. Quick, what would Nancy do?

As you glance around, you notice that the auditorium doors are open and no one is inside. So you silently walk behind Lisa until you get to the open door, then you slip inside and slide down into the nearest seat, hoping your head isn't visible over the back of it. Nancy would be proud.

The girls spend the next few minutes discussing all the movies they want to see and sales at the mall they want to hit. Yawn. *When are they going to get to the juicy stuff?* you wonder. And as if you had asked that question out loud, Maria's next words confirm your worst fears.

"Can you believe Mr. Carber?" you hear Maria complain

while her locker creaks open. "Giving us all that math homework on a Friday? What's his problem anyway?"

You hear another creak and the thud of books being slammed onto a metal shelf. "Who knows? He must hate kids or something. Weekend homework is just cruel and unusual punishment."

So far nothing you disagree with there. Mr. Carber is known around school as the weekend ruiner. "Speaking of cruel and unusual punishment, how are we going to deal with that girl Jessie?" Maria continues.

"Shh!" Lisa warns. "Keep it down! We don't want the whole school to hear."

"Sorry," Maria answers. "But you heard her singing that Miley song. She doesn't sound half bad. And if she actually beats out Mona for a solo, Mona is going to be a drag to be around for the rest of the year."

Lisa shuts her locker and lowers her voice even more, making you strain to hear. "I know. Relax. I already have the perfect plan."

"Of course you do!" Maria cries in honest admiration. "I should have known. So what is it?"

There's a pause—probably Lisa doing a quick check over each shoulder to see if anyone's listening. Good thing she doesn't think to check the auditorium!

"Well, you saw how quickly Jessie jumped at the chance to have lunch with us, right?"

"Totally. It's like she's desperate to upgrade out of her own loser clique."

"Exactly," Lisa confirms. "Which means she's like putty in our hands. She'll do whatever we say, as long as we make her think she's one of us. So all we have to do is give her some really, really, *really* bad advice for the audition. I bet she'd sing the *Barney* theme song if we told her to."

They're lucky you're in hiding, because your fists are clenched in fury and there's no telling what you'd do if you could break cover. That's your friend they're talking about! The nerve of them!

"Yeah, but even she wouldn't fall for that. Hmm . . . Let's see . . . ," Maria mutters, the wheels in her brain working overtime.

"Hey! Didn't Amy tell us that Jessie was originally going to sing that Taylor Swift song but that it was way too high for her?"

"Oh, that would be perfect! It must be way out of her range! If we can just get her to sing that instead of the Miley song, she'll humiliate herself onstage, and Mona will have the solo handed to her on a silver platter."

"Genius," Lisa declares. "Maybe we can even get her to wear something stupid, just to put the whole thing over the top. But we'd better hurry. What do you say we go find our new best friend?"

You hear two locker doors slam shut, and the girls go giggling down the hall.

Finally! Your back was starting to cramp in your super-sleuth position. But no time to dwell on that. You've got to find Jessie, fast! Someone has to warn her about her new "friends."

Two more periods go by before you spot Jessie bending over the water fountain on your way to gym class.

"*Hey!* I've been looking all over for you!" you shout, clapping her on the back.

She probably would have been happy to see you too, if she weren't so busy gurgling. You kind of pushed her into the water-fountain stream by accident. Oops.

As she slowly backs away from the fountain, dripping water from her face and all over her shirt, her mouth hanging open in shock, you can practically see the steam shooting out of her ears. (Especially when Celia and Delia walk down the hall, see Jessie, and start snickering.)

"This had better be good," she snaps. "I just got this top from H&M and now it's soaked!"

"Um . . . well, maybe you can say it's the new style? You know, water-fountain chic," you offer.

Jessie smirks at you. She is *so* not buying that one. Better just change the subject.

"All right, sorry," you tell her, "but I do really need to talk to you. It's about the audition."

"Oh!" she says, brightening up immediately. Suddenly even her blond ponytail seems to have a little more bounce. "Why didn't you say so? Maria and Lisa had some fabulicious ideas—"

"I'll bet they did," you interrupt, sucking your teeth.

Jessie stops and crosses her arms, jangling with her customary armload of bangles. "What's with the 'tude?"

It's time to lay it all on the line. She won't want to hear this, but it's better that she get the news from you now than to realize the truth while she's making a ginormous (as she would say) fool of herself onstage.

"Look, Jess, I hate to tell you this, but Lisa and Maria aren't who you think they are. They aren't really planning to initiate you into their 'it-girl' ranks. They just want you to *think* they are so that you'll do whatever they want for the audition and blow it big-time." As quickly as you can, you fill her in on the whole conversation you "accidentally" overheard by the lockers—leaving out the more hurtful things they said about your bud.

There is a moment of silence when Jessie is just staring at you while kids shuffle past the two of you on their way to class. "Wow," she says finally. "I don't believe it."

"I know! It's crazy. I didn't think they would stoop that low either. But now we've got to—"

"No," says Jessie, interrupting you this time. "I can't believe *you*. You were too chicken to audition, so now you make up all these lies because you're jealous."

You're a smart cookie, but right now you're feeling downright dense. Did she just accuse you of lying to her? Even worse, did she just accuse you of lying because you're *jealous*? In your mind you work up an intelligent, well-thought-out response to Jessie. "Huh?"

"You heard me," she says quickly, looking a little uncertain but determined to stick to her guns. "You're just jealous because I was brave enough to sign up for the audition, and now even Lisa and Maria think I'm cool." She raises her chin defiantly, so you can almost see straight up her nose.

UNREAL! Not the fact that you can see up her nose. (That you've seen lots of times.) But the fact that she doesn't believe you. You and Jessie have been friends since you were five years old and you've never lied to her about something so important. You even told her when her candy dish made out of dried macaroni looked more like a plateful of worms. So how could she think you'd lie to her now?

"You've gotta be kidding me!" you cry. "I was just looking out for you, but if this is how you're gonna be, fine! You're on your own."

"Fine." Jessie shrugs.

"Fine!"

"Fine!" you both shout in unison.

Without looking back, you head off to gym class, leaving Jessie and her wet H&M shirt and thick head behind. The nerve of her! Okay, maybe you do kind of wish you'd had the guts to audition. But Jessie should know you would never sabotage her shot at success, and you definitely wouldn't lie to her—which is more than you can say for her new so-called friends. But now that she seems to have fallen under the in-crowd's spell, she's going to follow their terrible advice and get herself laughed off the stage.

Just as you have this thought, you realize you are passing by the sign-up sheets. You notice that there is one slot left on the student-judge side. You know that if you were one of the judges, Jessie would have a chance. Even if you couldn't convince anyone else to vote for her, she would at least get your vote, so she wouldn't suffer the embarrassment of being totally dismissed. But right now, your hand is shaking so hard with anger that you aren't even sure you can pick up the pen.

There are times you're a little too skeptical for your own good, but this wasn't one of those times. For once your instincts were right: Lisa and Maria aren't really Jessie's biggest fans. They're just setting her up for a fall so that Mona can grab the big prize and they won't have to deal with her sore-loser attitude. Luckily, you were able to find that out before Jessie did anything stupid. But not only didn't Jessie believe you, she thinks you said those things because you're jealous. Jealous! Unbelievable. You were only trying to be a good friend and this is the thanks you get? Part of you wants to sign up as a student judge so that you can help her anyway. The other part wants to let her crash and burn to teach her a lesson about who her real friends are. After the way she just acted, you're tempted to let her go down in flames. You might be too hotheaded to know if you would really do that or not—so take the quiz to find out for sure.

QUIZ TIME!

Circle your answers and tally up the points at the end.

1. **Your favorite band is finally coming to your town and you scored two tickets through a radio contest. You offer your extra ticket to your best friend and she's totally psyched. But the night before, your crush calls and says he heard about your extra ticket and would love to go with you. What do you do?**

   A. Take your best friend, of course! It's not even a question. You already promised her the ticket and no way would you choose anyone over her—even if he does have the world's deepest dimples.

   B. Tell him you really wish you could, but you're already taking your friend, who might defriend you if you dump her for him. But you offer to bring him back a T-shirt.

   C. Agree to ask your friend if she wouldn't mind backing out. You'll feel kind of crummy (because, duh, of course she'll mind!), but surely she'll understand that this is your big chance to spend some quality time with your crush. If she says no, though, you'll deal.

   D. Break the news to your friend that you have to take your crush instead. Going to the concert with your BFF would have been fun and all, but you see her all the time. If she's a real friend, she'll get over it and be happy for you.

2. **You are at a school dance that is being chaperoned by some of the parents. When a group of older kids point out the geeky twosome**

busting some old-school moves on the dance floor, you realize with horror that they're talking about your mom and dad! When someone asks whose parents they are, you:

A. step up to claim them right away—and dare anyone to say anything else about them. Your folks may in fact be total dorks (your dad *is* trying to moonwalk, after all), but they're *your* dorks and you won't stand for anybody bad-mouthing them—besides you, that is.

B. admit that they're technically your parents, but you suspect you may have been adopted. You wouldn't want anyone to think the geek gene had been passed down to you.

C. sneak away without a word and spend the rest of the night hiding behind the punch bowl. You don't want to publicly disown them since they are family, but you also don't want anyone to notice the resemblance between you and the couple doing the robot on the dance floor.

D. claim that they must be escapees from a local mental ward who crashed the party. If you could, you would have security escort them out before they cause someone (namely, you) to die of embarrassment.

3. You have moved to a new town and made new friends. When a pal from your old neighborhood comes to visit, she's a tad overwhelmed by all the new people in your life and acts a little brattier than she normally would. You know it's just because she's feeling insecure, but after she leaves, your new friends verbally tear her to shreds. You react by:

A. defending your old friend and telling your new buds that if they don't like her, that's just too bad, because the two of you are a package deal.

B. acknowledging that your buddy was not her usual charming self, but explaining that it's hard for her to see you with a new group of people she doesn't know. If they give her another chance, you know they'll come to love her the way you do.

C. changing the subject altogether. Your friend's oddball behavior kind of embarrassed you in front of your new crew, but that doesn't mean you want to hear them put her down.

D. trashing her right along with your new friends. If this is how she's going to act every time you make other friends, then she deserves it. Plus, defending her might only make the new girls shy away from you.

4. **Your sister has been dealing with some bullies at school and today she has decided to face them instead of running away. So of course you:**

A. face them right along with her. Whoever has a problem with your sis has a problem with you. You'll stand by her no matter what happens.

B. watch her face them from afar and vow to intervene if it looks like she can't handle it by herself. You want to support your sister, but there's no need for you to get involved unless you have to.

C. tell her to let you know if she really, really needs you as backup. Otherwise you're going home and wishing her the best.

D. head straight home and urge her to do the same. No way are you confronting those girls. (They're older, taller, and just plain mean.) If your sister insists on facing the bullies, she's on her own!

5. It is game four of the Little League World Series and your favorite team is on the verge of defeat. Everyone you know has started rooting for the longtime champs, who are leading the series. But you've always rooted for the team that is, unfortunately, losing big-time. When you find yourself in the stands during what could be the final game, you:

A. root for your team! Yes, you're the only one cheering them on, but you're no fair-weather fan. The other spectators might make fun of you for rocking the losing team's jersey and doing a one-person wave in their honor, but you want them to know they have at least one loyal supporter, win or lose.

B. quietly root for your team, but don't make a big fuss about it. You hope they win, but you don't want to draw too much attention to yourself. Isn't it enough that you're rooting for the underdog?

C. reluctantly cheer on the winning team. Yes, you secretly hope that your team will score a major upset, but chances are they won't.

D. switch allegiances and root for the champs along with everyone else. It gets boring cheering for a team that never wins. You want to be on the winning side for once!

Give yourself 1 point for every time you answered *A*, 2 points for every *B*, 3 points for every *C*, and 4 points for every *D*.
   —If you scored between 5 and 12, go to page 145.
   —If you scored between 13 and 20, go to page 153.

chapter NINE

What a trusting soul you are! Because you tend to be honest with the world, you assume everyone else is too. You don't see why anyone would lie, so you take people at their word and buy everything you see in the media—hook, line, and sinker. It's great that you are so open and willing to give others the benefit of the doubt. But watch out! As hard as it is for you to believe, there are some out there who will try to take advantage of your naive nature. Don't be afraid to ask questions and make sure that what you see is really what you get.

Gym class is usually one of your favorite times of the day. But right now, you definitely feel off your game. Anyone would feel the same if they were seeing the scene you're watching right now.

Instead of Jessie standing by your side as usual, ready to

take on any volleyball challengers together, she's milling around on the other side of the court chatting with Shawna, Dionne, and Adam. Jessie says something you can't hear and the other three start laughing like whatever she said is the funniest thing they've ever heard in their life.

And just as Adam starts to look your way, you drop to one knee and focus on tying and retying your sneakers. You've always thought Adam was pretty cute with his golden blond hair and hazel eyes. Even in his gym sweats, he manages to look preppy but cool. It's hard to look away, but you just wouldn't be able to stand having him catch you staring at their little group, or at him. You need some time to process this change of routine. Jessie, apparently, is popular now. That part isn't really too surprising. After all, you've always known how awesome Jessie is; you guess it was only a matter of time before the A-listers caught on. But still, watching them together (and noting that Jessie doesn't even attempt to call you over to join them), you can't help feeling left out.

Thankfully, the phys ed teacher, Mr. Nocera, walks in then, carrying several volleyballs in his arms. Ordinarily, Jessie would choose that moment to whisper in your ear for the millionth time about how Mr. Nocera looks like a slightly older Taylor Lautner. And you would say no way. He looks more like the guy who plays Damon in *The Vampire Diaries*. And you'd debate about it until it was time to start kicking some volleyball booty. You're sure Jessie will remember your routine . . . any second now. Yep. She's about to come over to you right . . . now! Um, now?

Okay, she's not coming over. Instead, she's whispering into Shawna's ear and Shawna is nodding enthusiastically. If you didn't know Jessie better, you'd say she was sharing your special routine with someone else. But that can't be — can it?

Before Mr. Nocera chooses the captains for the day, Shawna raises her hand with a big grin on her face while Jessie stands next to her, wide-eyed and horrified.

"Yes?" Mr. Nocera says smoothly to Shawna while bouncing one of the volleyballs to make sure it isn't flat.

"Sir, Jessie and I were just wondering if you'd seen the *Twilight* movies by any chance. You know, the ones with Taylor Lautner?" Shawna says, holding back a huge smile. Jessie hides her face behind Shawna's back.

Mr. Nocera's eyebrows knit for a moment; then he starts tossing volleyballs to various kids around the gym. "No, can't say that I have. Why, should I?" he asks.

"Definitely," Shawna says. And finally she and Jessie are unable to hold back their giggles. It is the closest anyone has ever come to telling Mr. Nocera Jessie's theory. Looking over at Jessie, you can tell she is both embarrassed and in total awe of her new friends. So much so that when Mr. Nocera chooses Dionne as one of the captains and she picks Jessie to be on her team, Jessie actually squeals a little in delight.

For the first time, you'll be playing against your best friend.

To make matters worse, her team is stacked with most of the strongest players, while your team . . . well, Mary and Holly are your best assets, and only because they sometimes manage to hit the ball by accident while complaining about having to take gym class in the first place. (Sigh . . .)

You are five minutes into the first game (and losing badly) when your turn to serve comes up. You toss the ball up into the air in a perfectly straight line and execute an expert overhand serve. You pride yourself on being able to deliver a serve that other teams have a hard time returning, mostly because you're good at spotting the places on the court where the other team doesn't have any players, and aiming right for those spots. Jessie always hailed you as a volleyball goddess for being able to pull that off.

Unfortunately, this time Jessie is on the opposite team, and when your serve makes its way like a bullet over the net, Jessie is there with her arms outstretched, moving quickly into the space that was completely empty just a second before. Without even batting an eyelash, she bumps the ball up right next to the net, where Dionne sets it like a pro for Adam, who then smashes it over the net for a killer spike.

Since you've got kneepads on, you dive, stretching out your arms in a desperate attempt to dig the ball away from the floor. But you're a second too late and the ball goes rolling out of bounds. Holly shrugs at you without moving a muscle to help you up. "Nice try," she says flatly and goes back to staring at her nails.

"Psst! Hey, you all right?" comes an urgent whisper from across the court. It's Jessie, having the decency to look concerned.

You nod, less hurt than mortified. "I'm fine."

"Are you sure?" Jessie continues. "That looked pretty bad."

"I said I'm fine!" you answer, barely hiding your annoyance. Bad enough your best friend in the world has defected to Planet Popular, but now she's drawing attention to your humiliation. For some reason, though, she doesn't pick up on your irritation at all. Instead she just says, "Okay, good!" She waves happily and then rejoins her team huddle to plan out their next play.

Needless to say, her team creams yours with a score of 15 to 3. (And one of those points happened only because Mary blocked a spike with her head—not on purpose— and it flew back over the net before the other team had time to react. Mary left right after to go see the nurse.)

Jessie, meanwhile, is celebrating her team's easy victory over your team of . . . well, let's just say your team won't be going for Olympic gold anytime soon. Since Jessie was able to return each one of your killer serves, they are hailing her as the MVP, and Adam and Kevin even attempt to lift her onto their shoulders before Mr. Nocera orders them to stop. (Can't have a girl cracking her head open on the gym floor.)

You are unusually quiet while you change back into your school clothes in the locker room. But Jessie chatters away excitedly. You're still adjusting your shirt when Shawna comes back into the locker room, having changed already, and says, "Hey, Jessie. Adam is waiting for you outside. He says he still needs to talk to you about . . . that thing?"

"Oh! Right, the thing!" Jessie says with a wink. When Jessie looks at you and your puzzled face, she explains quickly, "Audition stuff. I have to head out to the music room. I'll catch you later, okay?"

"Sure, okay," you submit, as if you have a choice.

"'Kay, later!" With that Jessie rushes off, shouting, "Hey, Dionne, wait up!"

Maybe you're being overdramatic, but you have a terrible feeling in the pit of your stomach that you are losing your best friend. Auditioning is one thing. But playing on their team? Sharing private jokes and flirting with one of your secret crushes? She didn't even wait for you to finish changing after gym like she usually does. You hope you're wrong, but this feels to you like the beginning of the end.

What happened? This morning, you and your two best friends were all on the same page. Jessie was just as gung ho about breaking up the cliques as you were. But now she seems to be joining one instead. And what really hurts is that it looks like she has no intention of inviting you along for the ride. She is still talking to you and all, but she is having way too much fun with the in-crowd—including Adam, a guy she knows you think is pretty easy on the eyes. As far as you're concerned, this has gone too far. It feels like you should do something about it. Or should you let the chips fall where they may? Take the quiz to find out if you take action, or let it happen.

QUIZ TIME!

Circle your answers and tally up the points at the end.

1. **You're the editor of the school newspaper, and you have a ton of work to do if you want to get the paper out by the deadline. Your friends offer to help. Do you accept?**
    A. Uh-uh. No way, no how. They'd only mess it up, creating even more work for you. You'll get it done much faster on your own.
    B. Yes, but you watch all of them like a hawk, hovering over their shoulders. You insist on approving every little thing they do. They might not like it, but the paper is your responsibility and you have to make sure it comes out right.
    C. Sure, but you enlist one of your more reliable friends to keep an eye on what everyone else is doing while you finish up the layout. It makes you a little nervous to leave things up to anyone else, but you trust your pal to let you know if there are any problems.
    D. YES! You gratefully put them all to work before they have a chance to change their minds, and just pray they know what they're doing. You can use all the help you can get!

2. **When getting your hair done at the salon, what is your MO?**

    A. Salon? Please! You can't trust a stylist with your locks. You do your own hair at home. It's hard to imagine anyone else being able to do it right.

    B. Insist on sitting between two gigantic mirrors so that you can watch every single snip. One wrong stroke of the scissors and you're outta there.

    C. Rip a picture of a model sporting the cut you'd like out of a magazine, then give it to the hairstylist and let her work her magic. If you come out looking even half as good as the photo, you'll be pleased.

    D. Ask her to give you a great new look and don't even peek until she's done. She's a professional, after all. You're sure she'll turn you into a total hottie.

3. **Your birthday is coming up and you want it to be really special. What are you hoping for?**

    A. To plan everything yourself and then just invite people to your masterpiece. You're a great party planner, so you don't mind. Besides, if you leave it up to anyone else, you might not get what you want.

    B. To go over everything with your friends and family. You want to make all the final decisions, but you're happy to let them help.

    C. To let your friends plan everything while you kick back and watch. It's really fun to see them put everything into place—although you had to veto the strawberry cheesecake they wanted to order. Don't they know you're a chocoholic?

D. A surprise party! Not knowing where or when it's going to happen and even having the guest list be a total surprise is the best. Plus, less work for you!

4. **If someone were to look through your backpack right now, they would find:**

A. your pencils neatly arranged in pencil holders, all your books covered and labeled (arranged in size order, of course), and your notebook color-coordinated by subject with assignments meticulously arranged. Organization is everything!

B. only the stuff you really need, with maybe a snack thrown in. If you keep it simple, it's much easier to find the things you're looking for when you need them.

C. kind of a mess during the week, but you usually clean it out over the weekend.

D. a total wreck! You're amazed you can find anything in there.

5. **When you're on the treadmill at the gym, you prefer to:**

A. keep it on manual and choose your own exercise regimen. You want to be in control of which workouts you do and how long you do each one. And you definitely want to set your own pace.

B. keep it on manual most of the time but also select a routine or two. You like being in charge of your own workout, but it doesn't hurt to try some stuff you're not used to doing.

C. pick a routine for most of your workout, but tone it down if you find it to be too hard. That's the great thing about having a machine instead of a real person as your personal trainer: You can just turn it off whenever you want!

D. randomly select a workout program and follow it, no matter how hard it is. That way after a while you'll be prepared for anything!

Give yourself *1* point for every time you answered *A*, 2 points for every *B*, 3 points for every *C*, and 4 points for every *D*.

   —If you scored between 5 and 12, go to page 203.

   —If you scored between 13 and 20, go to page 216.

chapter
TEN

You're aiming for the top of the social ladder and you won't stop until you get there! Yes, sometimes that means ditching longtime friends or bailing on responsibilities, but you feel that the end justifies the means. Your desire to be seen at the coolest places, with the coolest people, doing the coolest things is certainly understandable. Who wouldn't want to experience the fabulous life for a change? But you might want to be careful about who you step on to get there, since you might see them again on your way back down. And losing friends who have less flash but more substance isn't cool at all.

You're sitting right smack in the middle of Planet Popular—and you like it. This might be the first time ever that you've had lunch with Shawna Levin, Dionne Williams, Steven Oh, Adam Arap, Lisa Topple, and Maria Santos. You do feel kind of bad about blowing off your usual friends—especially Jimmy, who is shooting confused looks your way—but you just *had* to join your fellow judges. They might need to discuss important audition stuff—your choosing to sit with them is strictly business.

Well, okay, maybe not entirely. It turns out the grass really is a little bit greener on this side of the lunchroom. For starters, their table is right by the window, so the whole section is bathed in sunlight (instead of the sick fluorescent stuff you and your friends have to settle for on the other side of the caf). And all that light helps you to see the super-cute Adam Arap, who is sitting right across from you adjusting the sweep of his light blond hair every few minutes and then drumming his slim fingers against the table. He barely speaks, but he seems to be moving constantly. (*Maybe he plays the drums*, you think, and that's why he's always drumming his fingers against things. He's probably in a band and one day you're going to see him performing on MTV's Video Music Awards. And now you'll be able to say, *Yeah, I used to eat lunch with that guy.* How cool is that?)

"All right," Shawna calls out, interrupting your daydreams, "if you can all look away from your mystery-meat cheeseburgers for a minute . . ." She pushes away her lunch tray with a look of mock disgust, which makes Dionne laugh. ". . . We should really come up with a list of criteria to judge the singers who are going to audition today."

"Ooh, 'criteria,'" Steven says, adjusting his red baseball hat, which teachers are constantly making him take off during class. "Big word, brainiac. Did you learn that on *Sesame Street*?" With his shoulder he nudges Adam, who smiles with only one corner of his mouth, just like Kris Allen from *American Idol*. Adam gives Steven a big high five. Then he runs his hands through his hair again, gives the table a quick *tap-tap-tap*, and slowly blinks his sleepy-looking hazel eyes.

Shawna doesn't look fazed at all. Without missing a beat, she replies smoothly, "No, I got it from this thing called a *book*. We can't all spend every waking minute playing Madden Football. Some of us actually have to *read*." She says that last word with the same exaggerated look of disgust that she gave the cheeseburger, and then she gives the boys a wide smile.

"Hey, I'm not always playing Madden," Steven protests.

"No, you're right," Shawna answers sincerely. "Sometimes it's Zombie Warriors."

With that the whole table cracks up, and Steven stands, takes off his hat, and does a minibow to Shawna, admitting defeat. You're starting to see that having thrown the greatest party in the world over the summer is not the only reason Shawna is popular. She's confident and is always ready with a quick comeback for everything. She is your new hero.

"Can we get back to the list now?" Lisa Topple chimes in. "You know, while we're still young?"

"Right," Shawna says, pulling a spiral notebook with a scene from the latest *Twilight* movie out of her bag, followed by a purple pen. "Let's get started." At the top of the page she writes *Criteria* and below that a small purple *1*. "What kind of things will we be looking for as judges?"

"No BO," shouts Lisa, who is sitting next to you.

"If you're not gonna take this seriously—" Dionne begins.

"I am serious!" Lisa insists. "There's nothing worse than having to spend all that time in the choir standing next to someone who's never heard of deodorant. Am I right?" Lisa says to you, raising her auburn eyebrows.

You think solemnly for a moment. "Well, she does have a point. We don't want half the audience to pass out when our choir lifts the trophy in the air."

Across from you, Adam, who had been quietly eating his french fries all this time, actually laughs. He smiles his half smile at you and says, "Good one."

You made Adam laugh! He found something you said amusing! And he looked right at you too. You're so in. Good thing you're much too cool to geek out about it. Instead, you just nod as if to say, *I drop hilarious gems like that all the time. It's no biggie.*

"Okay, fine," Shawna says, taking up her pen to write. "Personal hygiene. Next?"

Maria, sitting next to Steven, raises her hand as if she's in class and waits for Shawna to point at her. "Well, *I* think we need to choose people who have some style. I mean, have you *seen* the gross outfits last year's choir wore? Lime green shirts and floor-length black skirts or khakis? Puh-leease!"

Dionne, who seems to be Planet Popular's voice of reason (aka their version of Lena), sighs and says, "Maria, I'm pretty sure the choir director is the one who chooses the outfits."

Maria folds her arms huffily. "Yeah, well, maybe if there were people in the choir who knew a thing or two about fashion, they could suggest a choir makeover to Mr. Parker and our school wouldn't have to look like a giant tennis ball in the competition."

That part you think Jessie would have in the bag. No way would she let any choir she was a member of hit the stage looking like they belonged at the U.S. Open. By the time Jessie was done with them, they'd all be ready for the red carpet instead of the green Astroturf.

Shawna nods begrudgingly. "That is true. All right. Number two: fashion sense. Let's move on to number three. I think we should look for showmanship."

"Showmanship?" Steven repeats. "You mean like someone who's going to tap-dance and juggle while they sing?"

"Noooo," Shawna says, throwing a french fry at Steven's forehead. "I'm just saying that whoever's singing the lead should grab our attention, you know?"

Steven shrugs.

"Do you know what I mean?" Shawna asks you, clearly looking for a little support.

"Totally," you answer quickly. "Even the best song on earth won't help if the person singing looks like a dead fish."

"Exactly!" Shawna exclaims. "I'm so glad you signed up to be a judge," she continues as she writes *NO DEAD FISH!!!* in big capital letters in the number-three slot. "You get it."

You try not to let the compliment go to your head, but you can't help it. You feel your face light up as you grin at your half-eaten pizza.

After Shawna underlines the no-dead-fish rule three times, she looks up at Adam. "You've been pretty quiet. What do you think we should look for?"

Adam makes a quick swipe through his hair and *tap-tap-tap*s the table, looking uncomfortable at having been put on the spot. "Uh . . . yeah . . . this might be too obvious but, how 'bout somebody who can sing good?"

Well, you can practically hear Lena correct Adam in your head. *Sing* well.

But Shawna doesn't correct him at all. She simply nods enthusiastically and says, "Now you're talking. Unfortunately, that's not too obvious at all. Some people around here seem to think all they need to do is open their mouths and scream out any ol' Disney tune and they're in."

There are two seconds of silence when everyone at the

table looks at one another before blurting out, "Mark!" all together. The table erupts in giggles. You feel bad laughing about Mark behind his back, but he's been killing everybody with his *Little Mermaid* one-man show. Besides, the fact that these kids have been having the exact same conversation you had this morning with Lena and Jessie makes you see that you and your crew are not so different from the kids who live on Planet Popular after all.

You've always thought of Shawna as this untouchable girl, too cool to even talk to. But it turns out she's pretty down to earth and friendly. Actually, they all are. And they seem to like you too. You haven't gotten a single dirty look or snide comment about how you belong over on the misfits' side of the lunchroom. Could it be that you've misjudged them all this time? Could an invite to their parties be far behind?

Just when you're beginning to indulge in a daydream about your social ranking getting a major upgrade, Lisa clears her throat to interrupt the laughter. "A-h-h-hem! Aren't you guys forgetting something? Mona is competing. So I don't know why we're bothering with a list of cri-te-ri-a"—she rolls her eyes sarcastically—"when I'll be voting for Mona no matter what, and you should too."

Okay, you did not see that one coming. And it could be your imagination, but you feel like Lisa directed that last part especially at you. "Whoa, whoa, whoooa," Dionne says, holding up her smooth brown hands. "I don't remember agreeing to that." But looking around the table, you see some nervous shifting, and no one is exactly rushing to say that they haven't at least thought about just handing the solo spot to Mona.

"If you've got any brains you will," Maria continues. "Lisa's right. If you don't want to deal with Mona and her major 'tude for the rest of the year, you'll vote for her. She never does any after-school stuff because she's so busy modeling, but she got special permission for this. She even skipped lunch today so she could go practice. She expects to win. You know how she is."

The miserable looks on all their faces say that yes, they know exactly how Mona is. And so do you.

"I would think you at least would be smart enough to vote for Mona and try to get on her good side," Lisa says to you.

Maria moves her tray out of the way so that she can lean in closer across the table. "Yeah. We heard you stole Jimmy from her over the summer. And didn't you try to steal her modeling job too?"

Your jaw drops open. ".What? It—I—It wasn't like that at all!" You didn't steal any modeling job from Mona. Yes, a model scout did approach you in the mall over the summer, but you didn't exactly drop out of school to become Heidi Klum. And you didn't steal Jimmy. It isn't your fault that he and Mona had a big fight before Shawna's birthday party, or that you and Jimmy have become friends since then. But you can tell by the curious stares on Shawna's and Adam's faces that it would be pretty pointless to try to explain what really happened.

Maria shrugs. "Maybe not," she says a little too sweetly. "But I guarantee you that's how Mona sees it. So if I were you, I'd vote with us. Mona is so much easier to get along with when she gets what she wants."

True. But still, you don't think it's fair to reward Mona for being a bully. And you definitely don't think it's right to decide to vote for her before the audition has even started — although that's totally what you were thinking of doing for Jessie.

You look over at Shawna to see what she's going to say, and she and Dionne start debating about the pros and cons of voting for Mona. But all you can think about is Jessie walking into a contest that's been fixed. Almost as if Lisa is reading your mind, you overhear her whisper to Maria, "At least we know Jessie won't be any competition for Mona. I can't even believe she bought it when we told her she sounded great this morning. I mean, did you hear her?"

"Yeah, she sounded like a hyena!" Maria laughs meanly.

You feel your fists clench and the heat rise on your neck. They must have been listening when you asked Jessie to give you a preview of her audition. You're just about to tell them off for lying to your friend . . . when you realize that you did the same thing. When Jessie sang for you earlier, you smiled in her face and told her she sounded awesome even though nothing could have been further from the truth. You droop in your seat like a wilting flower. Suddenly the grass on this side of the lunchroom isn't looking so green after all.

Some friend you are. First you back out of auditioning, forcing Jessie to pick up your slack. Then you lie to her about her singing abilities. Then to top it all off, you ditch your real friends (even Jimmy!) at lunch in order to sit with the in-crowd. Sure, you can tell yourself you just wanted to get to know your fellow judges, but the truth is that you saw a chance to climb up the social ladder and you took it. Yes, you did enjoy feeling like part of the gang and even having the incredibly cute Adam acknowledge your existence. But was it worth it? You are now being pressured to vote for Mona, of all people, and Lisa and Maria are trashing Jessie in the process. And you're not even defending her! Right now, you could be placed firmly in the frenemy camp, a place you never thought you'd be. But what do you do now that you're here? Should you follow the crowd, keep Jessie in the dark, and vote for Mona in hopes of getting on her good side and securing your spot in the cool clique? Or should you risk your newfound status by blazing your own trail? Take the quiz and find out what you would *really* do.

QUIZ TIME!

Circle your answers and tally up the points at the end.

1. You're browsing online for some new songs to add to your iPod playlist. How do you go about getting new music?

    A. Go on iTunes and download whatever is on the "Best-sellers" list.

B. Ask all your friends what you should download and then follow their advice. They know what you should listen to.

C. Listen to your friends' collections and download only the songs you love. Some of the songs are great, but some are just weird!

D. Listen to a bunch of stuff you've never heard and find something new that even your most hipster friends don't know about.

2. **Tomorrow is a school trip and your crush will be there. You want to look great. So you:**

A. wear whatever *Teen Vogue* says is hot, no matter how crazy it looks. They're the professionals, after all.

B. call all your friends to find out what they're wearing and model your look after theirs.

C. wear the typical teen uniform: jeans and a T-shirt. But add a twist, like a colorful shrug or cowboy boots.

D. wear what you always wear. You want your crush to like you for who you really are—vintage tees and all.

3. **In gym class, the other kids always want you on their team because:**

A. you tend to come up with the best plays and have no problem getting your teammates to follow your lead. With you as the captain, your team usually scores a win.

B. you're great at taking the captain's play and making it even better.

C. you are the true definition of a team player. Even though you're not usually playing one of the star positions, you're good at following instructions.

D. although you may not take charge on the field, you do bring the refreshments.

4. **Which *Gossip Girl* character are you most like?**

   A. Blair Waldorf: She ruled her high school with an iron fist and tended to take the reins in any given situation.

   B. Serena van der Woodsen: Her buds influence her (and not always in a good way), but for the most part she does what she wants.

   C. Jenny Humphrey: Although she is trying to follow her own path now, she spent most of the early seasons desperately trying to be part of the popular clique and often did whatever they asked in order to fit in.

   D. Nelly Yuki: She doesn't quite have the confidence to take charge of the crew, but at least she's part of it.

5. **Your friends have had a fight with a girl in your class who you've always gotten along with. They know you're her friend too, but they demand that you pick a side. The only sane thing seems to be to:**

   A. tell your friends you're sorry they feel that way, but you're going to hang with whoever you want. No one is going to boss you around and tell you who you can talk to. If they're your real friends, they'll agree.

   B. negotiate a truce between the girls instead. You're sure if you can get them in the same room at the same time and force them to talk, they can work it out.

C. steer clear of the girl when your friends are around, but be really nice to her when they aren't.

D. cross the girl permanently off your Facebook page. She seemed nice enough to you, but you can't go against your friends.

Give yourself 1 point for every time you answered **A**, 2 points for every **B**, 3 points for every **C**, and 4 points for every **D**.

—If you scored between 5 and 12, go to page 145.
—If you scored between 13 and 20, go to page 153.

chapter
ELEVEN

Social climbing doesn't interest you at all. Instead of constantly being on the lookout for a more popular friend or a better party, you're happy being exactly who you are and hanging with your close-knit group of buds. You may not ever be in the middle of the action, but you know that wherever your true friends are is the coolest place to be.

As you take your seat between Jimmy and Lizette, across from Charlie, Lena, and Jessie, you wave quickly over at Shawna, hoping she'll understand that you've got to sit with your crew. Shawna's pretty nice about it too. She just shrugs, then smiles and waves back before becoming absorbed in whatever it is the in-crowd talks about when they're together. Maybe you should have taken the time to get to know your fellow student judges, but today has been pretty stressful already, and nothing calms you down like some quality time with your friends.

Besides, you never pass up a chance to sit next to Jimmy—especially today, when he seems to actually need some encouragement.

"So are you ready for your big art debut, Picasso?" Jessie asks him as she reaches up to tighten her ponytail.

Jimmy just pushes his string beans back and forth on his tray, looking miserable. "Uh . . . not really. But I guess it's too late to back out now, right?"

"Back out?" you pipe up. "Why would you do a crazy thing like that?" As the words leave your mouth, you hope that Jessie and Lena don't bring up the fact that you backed out of the audition today. Better keep Jimmy talking. "You've been getting ready for this for weeks. What's the prob?"

"I don't know." Jimmy shrugs one shoulder and takes a big gulp of chocolate milk, then wipes away a few drops that fell on his shirt, which is already covered in small gobs of paint. "I'm afraid nobody will come. But I'm more afraid that *everybody* will come and think my paintings are lame."

"What? That's so not possible," you assure him. "You're the best artist I know. Everything you do is so awesome, and . . ." Immediately you feel the blood rush to your face as embarrassment creeps over you. Your friends all know that you have a big crush on Jimmy, but you don't exactly want to broadcast it by gushing about how great he is. Sheesh. Get it together! "Ahem. I mean, you'll be fine."

Jimmy smiles shyly at you, his dark green eyes barely meeting yours. "Thanks."

Lena gives Charlie a knowing grin but goes back to eating her fries without saying a word, thank goodness. You really hope none of this shows up in her blog later.

"Right," Jessie says. "And if it makes you feel any better, I'm nervous too."

"You are?" Jimmy asks, casting a doubtful glance at Jessie. "About what?"

"Haven't you heard?" Jessie says, her blue eyes widening in shock. You're all so used to Amy Choi spreading around every little tiny bit of school news that Jessie is clearly surprised that word of her signing up hasn't reached Jimmy yet. "I'm going for a solo in the choir today!"

"There are choir auditions today?" Jimmy asks with a blank expression.

"Uh, yeaaah," Jessie answers, as if Jimmy had just asked if Miley Cyrus and Hannah Montana are the same person. It's just one of those facts that everyone should know, as far as she's concerned. "And the closer we get to them, the more nervous I get. I just wish I knew what to expect!"

"There's no reason to be nervous, Jess," Lena says calmly. "Charlie has interviewed most of the faculty judges, and I have interviewed half the people auditioning, and they're all just as clueless."

"Hey!"

Lena pats her shoulder. "Oh, you know I mean that with love."

"Yeah, yeah," Jessie says, smirking at Lena.

"Besides," Charlie cuts in while straightening his tie. "At least you have one friend on the judging panel." He nods at you. "So it's not like you'll walk out of there with no votes."

"That's right, girl!" Lizette squeals, reaching over to bump fists with you. "We've got your back."

"That's true," Jessie says, instantly looking more cheerful. "This will be a piece of cake!"

As your friends go on talking about the blog and the audition and the art show, you can't help feeling like the lunchroom is getting smaller and smaller, making it hard for you to breathe.

Although none of them would come right out and tell you to vote for Jessie, that's obviously what they all think you'll do. But if your other friends had only heard Jessie sing this morning, they'd know that Jessie shouldn't automatically get your vote. Your only hope is that the other people auditioning all sound like Mark Bukowski (in other words, like nails on a chalkboard).

Finally the bell rings and everyone starts to file out of the cafeteria. You've never been so grateful to get lunch over with in your life! Even sitting next to your übercrush, Jimmy, couldn't salvage the last half hour.

Your friends have all gone ahead to their classes, and

you're drifting down the hallway in a fog of stress and guilt when all of a sudden you bump into someone in a pink Gap T-shirt and denim skirt.

"Oh! S-sorry, sorry," you stammer, trying desperately to pull your head out of the haze you've been in since you left the cafeteria.

"No problem," Lisa says innocently. "We wanted to talk to you anyway."

"We?" Finally you glance around and see Maria closing in from behind. They are standing on either side of you, blocking your path. This can't be good. But for the life of you, you can't think of a single reason they would need to talk to you.

"We heard that you're going to be one of the judges for the choir auditions," Lisa says, jumping right in.

"Uh, yeah . . . ," you answer slowly, refraining from adding, *What's it to you?*

"That's great," Lisa says. "So I assume you know that Mona is going for the solo, right?"

Suddenly you feel like a rock just sank to the bottom of your stomach. The answer to Lisa's question is a big fat no. You were so worried about Jessie's audition, you hadn't noticed that Mona had actually signed up to compete against her. Perfect.

"I do now," you say, trying to sound cool. "So?"

Maria stares at you in surprise, shocked, you guess, that you dare speak to them like that. "So," she repeats. "So?"

Lisa puts a hand on Maria's shoulder and gives her a warning look, as if to say, *I'll handle this.*

"So," Lisa goes on in a voice as smooth as silk, "we're judges too, and we were just thinking about how much nicer Mona is when she's happy. Like when she gets a good grade on a test, or when the weather is really nice out, or . . . when she wins a competition. A singing audition, for example."

As what they're saying sinks in, your stomach starts doing somersaults. Great. You're getting it from both sides. It's bad enough that your friends expect you to vote for Jessie. Now the popular girls are pressuring you to vote for Mona? If only this were some kind of hidden-camera show and this was all a big joke. No such luck.

Lisa slides one arm around your shoulders. "And it's no secret that she hasn't been all that nice to you. Especially since you started hanging with Jimmy. Didn't she put gum on your chair once?"

"A few times," you correct her, getting irritated. "But who's counting?"

"Hmm . . . ," Lisa purrs. "I bet she'd stop doing that if she had something else to focus on."

You nod slowly. "Right. Like maybe singing in Carnegie Hall?"

"Wow, you catch on fast!" Maria says with a big smile.

"I knew you were smart," Lisa adds. "If everything goes well with this judging thing, we should totally hang out."

"Uh-huh," you mutter. "I should get to class now."

Without another word Lisa slips her arm back off your shoulder, and she and Maria smile their sweetest smiles and step to the side, each of them swinging an arm out in front of them to show you the way down the hall. The effect is beyond creepy.

As you rush past them and down the hall toward your next class, you hear Lisa yell after you, "Don't forget what we talked about!" As if you could.

Remember that rock and hard place you were between this morning? Well, it looks like you're back there again! Just when you thought you could relax around your lifelong friends, they make it pretty clear that they expect you to vote for Jessie—who you already know is no Mariah Carey. Then before you even have a chance to decide what to do about Jess, your fellow judges, Maria and Lisa, make it equally clear that they want you to vote for Mona, implying that your life at school will get a lot better if you do. Who knew you'd have to make up your mind about who to vote for before you've heard even one note at the auditions? A better question is, are you the kind of person who bows to this sort of pressure? You probably think you know, but maybe you should take the quiz and find out for sure.

QUIZ TIME!

Circle your answers and tally up the points at the end.

1. The night before your biology final, your friends decide that you should all go hang out at the mall and catch a movie, then spend the night at your friend Annie's house so that you can all study together. To be honest, you'd rather just go home and focus on the final, but your friends are practically begging you to come. What do you say?

   A. No way, no how. Uh-uh. Not a chance. Negative. Basically? No. You know for a fact that if you spend the day hanging out and then try to study with your pals at night, you'll end up doing less studying and more talking, which equals failing the final in horrifying fashion. Your buds can get Fs if they want to, but they can count you out.

   B. You know you shouldn't, but you agree to spend the day at the mall with them but opt out of the sleepover. A few hours of fun during the day couldn't hurt, right? You've got all night to cram.

   C. You agree to the outing on one condition: The group of you actually has to crack the books together, and not just the magazines. You have a bad feeling that it won't go quite that way and you'll end up struggling through the test. But you don't want your friends to think you're a drag.

   D. All you ask is what time you should be at the mall and what you should bring to the sleepover. Your friends don't seem that concerned about the final, so why should you be worried?

2. Your crush has taken you to eat at his favorite diner, Pop's Greasy Spoon. He's been dying for you to try their triple-decker chili

cheeseburger, which comes with a heaping plate of cheese fries and the world's thickest milk shake. Sounds great . . . except that you recently vowed to start eating healthy foods and working out. When the waitress comes around, you order:

A. a spinach salad and a glass of water. That might seem like it's the opposite extreme, but maybe it'll encourage your crush to swing a little more in that direction.

B. grilled chicken with a side of broccoli, a baked potato, and a glass of iced green tea. You can still have a hearty meal that won't be quite as bad for you. (Not to mention you won't end up with chili breath.)

C. a regular cheeseburger and a soft drink. And you'll eat a few of your crush's fries. The triple-decker might be too much for you, but you want to prove to your date that you share his love of diner food. You can always go for a jog later.

D. the triple-decker chili cheeseburger, cheese fries, and extra-thick milk shake, of course! Yes, it will totally derail your plan to eat healthy stuff, but you don't want to let your crush down by having him face the triple-decker alone.

3. Though it has never been your thing, some of the girls at school have started wearing makeup. When a few of your classmates tell you that you look a little plain and offer you some blush, you respond by:

A. saying "No, thanks" and explaining to them that you

wouldn't want to ruin your complexion. You'll take plain and smooth over colorful and splotchy any day.

B. turning them down, but saying the blush looks good on them. You add that they looked just fine without it too.

C. saying "Okay, I guess" and letting them put a little blush on you. (You can always wipe it off later when they aren't around.)

D. shouting "Sure!" and preparing for a minimakeover. If everyone else is wearing makeup, maybe you should too. What's a few pimples anyway?

4. **You and a few kids from your school are volunteering at the local nursing home over the winter break. You're the one who organized the group and you really dig spending time there. But after about half an hour, the other kids get bored and want to leave. When they tell you that you should all ditch the nursing home and go shopping instead, you say:**

A. "You guys go on without me. I'm staying." One of the older women there has the best stories. The other kids are missing out!

B. "I'll catch up with you in a little while." You want to stay until you finish your checkers game with Mrs. Lankford. Then you'll be happy to hit up some sales with the other kids.

C. "All right," reluctantly agreeing to go. But you promise your nursing home friends that you'll come right back.

D. "Let's go!" Even though you really want to stay, you act like you can't wait to leave just so the other kids won't think you're weird.

5. **Your BFF has the brilliant idea that the two of you should wear matching outfits on picture day. She's even picked out the clothes already. You think her idea has "dorks" written all over it. So when picture day rolls around, you:**

    A. tell your friend it was a sweet idea, but no way are you doing that. Your friendship has always been based on being individuals, and you want to keep it that way.

    B. tell her you would, but your mom already bought you your picture-day ensemble and she'd be mad if you didn't wear it. (That isn't entirely true, but your best bud doesn't need to know that.)

    C. agree to wear the same outfit, but bring an extra set of clothes to change into right after so that you don't have to go around looking like twins for the rest of the day.

    D. go with her idea, even though you spend the whole day feeling pretty silly.

Give yourself 1 point for every time you answered *A*, 2 points for every *B*, 3 points for every *C*, and 4 points for every *D*.

— If you scored between 5 and 12, go to page 208.
— If you scored between 13 and 20, go to page 153.

chapter TWELVE

You are a slacker with a capital S.
If there is an easy way to do something, you choose it every time. And you've never met a couch you didn't like. Not that slacking is always a bad thing. After all, your body and your brain do need a certain amount of rest to function properly. But you're getting enough rest for an entire soccer team! Once in a while, why not try to put in a little extra effort? You might be very proud of what you can accomplish when you challenge yourself.

By the looks of this library, it hasn't been cleaned since the wheel was invented. There are piles of books and paper everywhere, mounds of dust are collecting on the bookshelves and windowsills, and there are stacks of encyclopedias that need to be put back in order. Truth be told, it makes you tired just looking at it!

You sigh at the unfairness of this punishment. But hey, that's what you get for letting Mona trick you into texting in class. Oh well. You guess you'll start with the easiest thing: the pile of paper spilling over the reception desk. You halfheartedly gather a pile and stack it neatly before trying to figure out where each piece should go. You start to make separate piles, but pretty soon you forget which pile was for what, and you end up just moving the same pieces of paper from one pile to the other. You try to focus, honest. But you're much too busy fantasizing about all the ways you'd like to get back at Mona. Planting a hive of bees in her locker? Nah, too dangerous. Posting an ugly picture of her on Facebook? Eh, that wouldn't work. As evil as Mona is, she is also annoyingly pretty, with jet-black hair, deep blue eyes, and flawless skin. Even her teeth are perfectly straight. And the fact that she's a model makes it hard to catch a bad picture of her. She seems to always be prepared for the camera. Maybe if you—

"You're not going to get much done that way," a voice says from behind one of the stacks, interrupting your daydream. You realize now that for the past few minutes, you haven't even been shuffling paper. You were just resting your cheek on your hand and staring out the dusty window. According to the clock, you've already wasted most of your lunch period.

"Huh? Who said that?" you cry, a bit embarrassed at being caught slacking on the job.

"I did," the voice says again. Finally, you hear the squeak of a book cart being pushed by Joey Cruz. You couldn't be more shocked if you tried. Joey is a total rock star on the baseball team and is an all-around popular guy. The fact that his deeply tanned skin makes him look like he just got back from a sun-kissed beach certainly doesn't hurt. Not to mention he has a tall, lanky build, short black hair, and unusual light brown almond-shaped eyes. Even his eyebrows, which are a little bushy, and his slightly crooked bottom teeth make him seem mysterious. The best part about him, though, is that he seems completely unaware that half the girls in school are into him. You're used to seeing him walk around the halls with long, easy strides, in oversize T-shirts and baggy jeans, iPod earbuds in his ears, casually nodding to friends as he passes by. He always seemed friendly, just way too cool to ever be in the same place at the same time as you. You don't even have any classes with him. So what is he doing here in this dirty library—pushing around a book cart no less?

"H-hey," you stammer, caught completely off guard. "Were you texting in class too?"

"What?" he asks, tilting his head in confusion. Then you see understanding dawn on his face. "Ooh, I get it. You were sent here as some kind of punishment, yeah?"

"Yeah," you confirm. Being identified as a small-time

criminal is not exactly the first impression you hoped to make if you ever actually had a conversation with Joey. So much for that. "What about you? This isn't some weirdo form of baseball practice, is it? Because if I were you, I'd quit the team."

Joey throws back his head and laughs at that. To your surprise, even though he looks more like Derek Jeter, he has a deep, full laugh that makes him sound like Santa Claus. It's contagious. You can't help laughing too. As his laughter fades away, he shakes his head and points at you. "You're funny."

You raise your eyebrows in surprise. *I am?* you think. *Sweet!*

"Actually, I've been volunteering here a few times a week to take care of the library while Mrs. O'Donnell is on maternity leave."

"Really?" You don't mean to shout, but you never thought that really popular guys did nice things for others unless they were forced to.

"You don't have to sound so surprised," Joey says, seeming only slightly offended. "I know I'm a jock, but that doesn't mean I don't like books. Actually, Mrs. O'Donnell is the one who got me into science fiction. Some of it's really good. And she helped me out when I was having trouble with Shakespeare." He pauses, looking down quietly at his cartful of books, as if he is remembering all the kind things Mrs. O'Donnell has done for him. You never noticed before how cute a boy can be when he's being thoughtful and not so loud. Even the uneven dip in his chin suddenly seems more appealing. You only realize that you're staring at him when he turns his caramel eyes to the floor and starts rubbing the back of his neck.

Joey shrugs suddenly, snapping out of his thoughts. "Anyway, she's just always been really cool with me, so I figured the least I could do is try to keep the library in some kind of order while she's out. But"—he glances at the mess that is overwhelming the desk where you are sitting—"it's kind of a two-person job, yeah?"

You look down guiltily at your shuffled papers. "Ha-ha . . . yeah. Sorry about that. I guess I haven't exactly pulled my weight."

He laughs softly this time. "That's all right. Why don't you just help me reshelve these books?"

"Sounds like a plan."

For the next few minutes, you put books away in relative silence.

"You have a lot on your mind, yeah?" Joey asks after a while. "You're pretty quiet."

You reach to put a history book back on a shelf. "Sorry, I guess I'm just worried about this audition."

"That choir thing? Cool. Are you going for the solo?" For a moment, you're floored by the fact that Joey knows—or cares—about the choir auditions.

"Well, I was going to, but now I'm not sure."

"How come?" Joey asks. Wow, he actually seems interested in how you feel. Maybe you've been really wrong about the popular cliques.

"Well, you know Mona, right?"

Joey holds his hand up to his shoulder. "About this high, pretty face, mean streak?"

"That's the one!"

"Sure, I know her. Who doesn't?"

You kind of wish you didn't. But since you do, you go on to tell Joey everything that has happened since this morning: from signing up during homeroom, to history class, to ending up in the library—leaving out the part where you consider putting a hive of bees in Mona's locker. You might be guilty of misjudging Joey, but you know for a fact that you're not that far off base when it comes to Mona.

"Dude," Joey says when you're done. "Sounds like Mona really does have it in for you."

"I know!" you cry, happy to have someone confirm what you already believe. "So that's why I'm not even sure I feel like auditioning against her now. I'm thinking I might just skip it, you know?"

You fully expect Joey to support your dropping out of the audition. What else could he say after hearing your tale of woe?

"Not auditioning now would be so lame," Joey says matter-of-factly. Huh? Wasn't he supposed to be telling you how sorry he felt for you right about now, and saying that he would completely get it if you didn't want to deal with going up against Mona?

Seeing the look of outrage on your face, Joey grabs a nearby footstool and takes a seat, resting his hands on his thighs. "Look," he begins seriously, "Mona thinks she's got you on the ropes, so now you've *got* to audition. Otherwise she'll feel like she can scare you out of anything, yeah?" Jeez, even the way he says "yeah" all the time is cute. You wonder vaguely where he picked up that habit.

"Yes, but what if I do it and then she's even more evil to me than she was before? Or what if she—"

Joey cuts you off with an exaggerated yawn. "Boooring," he says.

Your mouth drops open. You're not used to anyone being so blunt with you. You kind of like it.

He stands up, puts his hands on your shoulders, and looks deeply into your eyes, giving you a chance to notice the wiry muscles beginning to develop in his arms, probably from hitting all those home runs. "Coach always tells us that if we want to win, we have to make up our minds to do it. That's what you've got to do!"

You peer at him, a little doubtful. "Just decide to win, huh?"

"That's it. But if you need some extra motivation," he says, leaning back, "how about I take you out after school if you actually go through with the audition?"

Joey never stops surprising you. You could be wrong, but you're pretty sure he just asked you out. For a brief moment, you want to hug Mona for getting you in trouble during history class. But thinking about her sends your mind reeling again. Can't anything today be easy?

The good news: You were brave enough to sign up to sing—even after you saw that auditioning meant going up against your archnemesis, Mona. The bad news: You let her bait you into a text-message war during class that got your phone confiscated and you sent to do hard labor in the library. And your inner slacker let the whole lunch period tick by without finishing the job, which means there was zero time to hunt down your teacher and beg for your phone. So you're still phoneless and have no idea what's going on with your friends. What you do know is that you've had baseball phenom Joey all wrong. Not only is Joey not a slacker (unlike *some* people you know), but he's a really nice guy and he's given you some much-needed tough love. He even asked you out, kind of. Sweet! It's tempting. But you promised you would go by Jimmy's art exhibit later, so you don't know if you can take Joey up on his offer. Besides, you still aren't sure you would stand a chance against Mona. Sometimes it's hard to find the silver lining when all you can see are dark storm clouds. So what to do? Take the quiz to figure out if you'll be able to see past all the problems and find the solution.

QUIZ TIME!

Circle your answers and tally up the points at the end.

1. **You are going to the hospital tomorrow to have your tonsils taken out. How do you feel?**

   A. Great. It would be silly to feel nervous. The surgery you're having is routine and no big deal. Plus you're pretty sure you'll get to eat your weight in ice cream and Jell-o over the next few days. You'll be just fine.

   B. You are understandably a little jittery. (After all, any surgery involves some risk.) But you know a bunch of people who've gone through it and they're all okay, so you probably will be too.

   C. You are kind of freaking out, even after asking your doctor a zillion questions. You trust him and all, but what if something goes wrong? (You may not be entirely sure what your tonsils do, but it can't be a good thing to have them removed.)

   D. You are in major panic mode. What if they take out your voice box instead of your tonsils and you can never talk again? Aaaaagh!

2. **You're reading an exciting new book and one of the chapters ends on a cliff-hanger with the main character in big trouble. Are you worried?**

   A. Not at all. You know she'll find some brilliant way out of the mess. She always does.

B. A little. She's in a real bind. But if anyone can find a way out, she can.

C. Definitely. You have no idea how you would get out of that jam. You doubt that she'll find a way, but since there is a small glimmer of hope, you read on and keep your fingers crossed.

D. Very. No way is she getting out of this one. You don't even bother reading the rest of the book because you can tell it won't have a happy ending.

3. **Your parents have planned a family cross-country trip in an RV. You think it'll be:**

A. awesome! You'll get to ride around in an RV, spend lots of time with your fam, and see all the different states. Plus you can send your friends goofy postcards from each stop. You can't wait!

B. okay. You're a little worried about getting cabin fever (and taking regular showers), but for the most part it'll be great. Anything that goes wrong will just make for some funny stories later.

C. fun part of the time, but really long car trips can be a drag. And to be honest, you'd rather lie out on the beach than see the Grand Canyon. But for your family's sake, you'll grin and bear it.

D. awful! You'll probably get motion sickness, your little bro is bound to get on your nerves, and you'll be away from your friends for weeks. If you could stay home, you would.

4. **Your best friend just told you she'll be moving away next month and is really upset about it. You tell her that:**

   A. you'll end up writing and talking on the phone even more than you do now! There will be so much more to talk about since you'll be at different schools. And you can always visit. Her move might actually bring you closer!

   B. the two of you can keep in touch through Facebook and Twitter. It won't be as good as getting to hang in person every day, but it's the next best thing.

   C. you'll stay in contact for a while, but it'll be too hard to keep in touch for long. So you'd better prepare yourselves for the inevitable.

   D. you'll probably never see or talk to each other again. People always say they'll keep in touch, but they never actually do. You might as well say your good-byes now.

5. **While riding your bike in the park, you fell and broke your leg—right before your prom! How do you feel?**

   A. Actually, you think it's pretty cool. All your friends will want to sign your cast, and making up dances that you can do on crutches might be funny. (All the attention and sympathy you'll get will just be icing on the cake.)

   B. Not too bad. It is terrible timing, but you know your friends will help you get around. And if you sit most of the night, no one will even notice that your cast clashes with your dress.

   C. It's kind of a bummer. You were really hoping to wear your cute kitten-heeled shoes, but you'll be wearing a huge clunky white cast instead. Still, it could have been worse. You could've broken both legs!

D. It stinks. There's no way you'll have a good time now, so you might as well skip it.

Give yourself 1 point for every time you answered *A*, 2 points for every **B**, 3 points for every **C**, and 4 points for every **D**.

—If you scored between 5 and 12, go to page 179.

—If you scored between 13 and 20, go to page 188.

chapter
THIRTEEN

good for you! You're no stranger to hard work and you don't mind putting in a little extra effort if it means a bigger payoff. You tend to do more than what is expected, making you a favorite of your teachers and anybody you work for, which is great. Just be sure to relax once in a while too. . . . Everyone needs some downtime to recharge their batteries.

Glancing around the library, you see you've got your work cut out for you. There are books piled up everywhere that need to be put away, there is a mountain of dust on each bookshelf, and the reception desk is buried under an avalanche of paper. It has only been a few weeks since the librarian, Mrs. O'Donnell, went on maternity leave, but already the place looks more like an ancient ruin than a modern library. Good thing you're always up for a challenge. This won't be any different from the millions of times you've reorganized your own room.

First you take on the easiest job to get it out of the way. You grab all the loose books floating around and put them back on the shelves where they're supposed to go. Thanks to the numbering system, that part is a piece of cake. Tackling the army of dust bunnies is tougher, but they're no match for the rag and lemon Pledge you find behind Mrs. O'Donnell's desk. With a little elbow grease, you have those shelves and the windows gleaming in no time.

Finally, you tackle the papers covering every inch of the reception desk, separating them into three piles: trash, file, or miscellaneous. Thankfully, the trash pile is pretty large, so you're able to recycle a ton of paper. And Mrs. O'Donnell's files are top-notch, so filing the second stack of paper doesn't take long at all. You are just straightening out the miscellaneous pile and arranging it neatly in Mrs. O'Donnell's in-box when you hear the squeak of a library cart. You've been so consumed in your work you didn't even realize that you weren't alone.

From inside the librarian's office, Joey Cruz comes into view, pushing a cartful of books toward you. Joey is even more popular than Shawna, partly because he is one of the biggest stars on the baseball team, and partly because he happens to be one of the best-looking guys in eighth grade.

For starters, he's a little taller than most of the other guys, and he has caramel-colored eyes that really stand out against his tan skin. Despite the fact that his eyebrows are kind of bushy and his bottom teeth are a little crooked, he is a bona fide school heartthrob—not that he seems to know it. He's usually too busy playing baseball, working on his batting stance, or listening to his iPod to notice anybody drooling over him. So what is he doing tooling around a dusty old library?

He scans the room quickly and then lets his mouth slack open in what you think is awe. "You—you did all this? Just now?"

You nod and look at your handiwork proudly. "Yep! Not bad, huh?"

"Not bad? Are you kidding? Dude, you rule! Mrs. O'Donnell is gonna flip when she gets back." He goes on to explain that the librarian has been so cool to him that he decided to repay her by volunteering to keep an eye on the library a few times a week, but it's a bigger job than he bargained for. Wow. You were acting like you had received the worst punishment on earth, and Joey was here helping out just to be nice. All this time you'd thought popular jocks like him didn't do anything without a cheering section behind them. If you hadn't gotten in trouble today, you never would have even known that Joey isn't like that at all. His status as a secret do-gooder is suddenly way more interesting to you than the fact that he's a hottie.

"Well, I'm glad I could help," you tell Joey, who is still

looking around and rubbing his neck in utter disbelief. "But I should get going. I've got a cell phone to rescue!"

You strike a superhero pose for a second and then fly out of the library as if you're Supergirl. Out of the corner of your eye, you see him grin, revealing a few crooked teeth. But you have no time to dwell on Joey's adorable smile. If you hurry, you can make it to the teachers' lounge before the lunch period is over.

When you barge into the teachers' lounge, Ms. Krell is just about to take a huge bite out of her tuna salad sandwich.

"Ms. Krell!" you shout a little too loudly, scaring your history teacher so badly that she drops her sandwich onto the table, sending squirts of tuna fish flying everywhere. Oops.

"Sorry," you mutter softly, wincing at your bad timing.

Ms. Krell regains her composure, though, calmly reaching for a napkin and wiping down the table. "Ah, yes, the girl who thinks texting is more important than learning history. I assume you are done with the cleaning assignment in the library?" She gives you an ice-cold glare that almost makes your teeth chatter.

"Y-yes, ma'am," you stutter. "And I just want to say that I'm really, really sorry. I know I shouldn't have been using my phone during class, and it'll never ever happen again."

"Hmph!" Ms. Krell grunts. "If I had a nickel for every time a student promised me that . . ." She trails off, maybe fantasizing about what she would do if she really did have all those nickels. You're guessing she would have enough for a luxury vacation in Paris. But you're still not convinced that teachers even exist outside of school, let alone in fancy hotels in France.

"I know, I know," you agree. "You'd be rich. But I really mean it." You cross your heart with your index finger and then hold up your hand as if taking an oath. Then you flash her what you hope is your sincerest smile.

Ms. Krell casts a cool, appraising eye over you, sizing you up. Apparently you pass the test, because she gives you a small nod and then reaches into her purse, pulling out your precious Sidekick. *Hello, old friend!*

You reach for it, but Ms. Krell snatches it away, holding it just out of your reach. "Before I give you this phone," she says stiffly, "I want you to understand that I am only giving it back because you are usually one of my best students, so I can only assume this infraction was caused by temporary insanity."

As Lena would say back when she was quoting Shakespeare all the time, *Temporary insanity, thy name is Mona!* You know better than to make a joke right now, though. You simply nod in agreement and stare at the green linoleum tile.

"Next time I won't be so lenient. Do I make myself clear?" She holds out the phone to you and you pocket it quickly, before she has a chance to change her mind.

"Yes, Ms. Krell. Thank you, thank you, thank you . . . you won't regret this!" you cry, backing out of the teachers' lounge.

Yes! You got past that temporary roadblock and you

have your phone back. Thank goodness too. You head to your next class, checking your phone as you walk, and it looks like you have missed a ton of messages. Most are pretty run-of-the-mill—Lena updating you on her latest blog interviewee, Jessie complaining about how cold it is in the girls' bathroom, Amy Choi begging you to confirm the rumor that you'd been expelled and enrolled in military school. You know, the usual. But one text stops you cold. It's from Lizette.

> Heard Mona will B singing U B
> Long w Me. Isn't that UR song?

What? Of course that's your song. This is no coincidence. Mona is obviously trying to steal your thunder. But how did she even know what song . . . ? Oh, that's right. You actually blabbed that info yourself when she started bugging you in history class. So *that's* what all the texting was about. She was just setting a trap for you, and you fell right into it. Perfect. If you didn't feel like a sucker before, you definitely feel like one now.

Mona wins again. Thanks to her, you had to spend your lunch period cleaning instead of eating and catching up with your buds. And even though that led to a brief encounter with the cute (and surprisingly

sweet) Joey, it also led to your having to grovel to get your phone back. But the worst had yet to come. Mona is planning to use your song for the audition! Since she signed up before you, she'll get to sing it first, which means you'll look like a lame copycat at best. Given the situation, is there any possible way this can work out for you? Your attitude could mean everything, so take the quiz to find out what that is.

QUIZ TIME!

Circle your answers and tally up the points at the end.

1. **You are going to the hospital tomorrow to have your tonsils taken out. How do you feel?**

   A. Great. It would be silly to feel nervous. The surgery you're having is routine and no big deal. Plus you're pretty sure you'll get to eat your weight in ice cream and Jell-O over the next few days. You'll be just fine.

   B. You are understandably a little jittery. (After all, any surgery involves some risk.) But you know a bunch of people who've gone through it and they're all okay, so you probably will be too.

   C. You are kind of freaking out, even after asking your doctor a zillion questions. You trust him and all, but what if something goes wrong? (You may not be entirely sure what your tonsils do, but it can't be a good thing to have them removed.)

   D. You are in major panic mode. What if they take out your voice box instead of your tonsils and you can never talk again? Aaaaagh!

2. **You're reading an exciting new book and one of the chapters ends on a cliff-hanger with the main character in big trouble. Are you worried?**

   A. Not at all. You know she'll find some brilliant way out of the mess. She always does.

   B. A little. She's in a real bind. But if anyone can find a way out, she can.

   C. Definitely. You have no idea how you would get out of that jam. You doubt she'll find a way, but since there is a small glimmer of hope, you read on and keep your fingers crossed.

   D. Very. No way is she getting out of this one. You don't even bother reading the rest of the book because you can tell it won't have a happy ending.

3. **Your parents have planned a family cross-country trip in an RV. You think it'll be:**

   A. awesome! You'll get to ride around in an RV, spend lots of time with your fam, and see all the different states. Plus you can send your friends goofy postcards from each stop. You can't wait!

   B. okay. You're a little worried about getting cabin fever (and taking regular showers), but for the most part it'll be great. Anything that goes wrong will just make for some funny stories later.

   C. fun part of the time, but really long car trips can be a drag. And to be honest, you'd rather lie out on the beach than see the Grand Canyon. But for your family's sake, you'll grin and bear it.

D. awful! You'll probably get motion sickness, your little bro is bound to get on your nerves, and you'll be away from your friends for weeks. If you could just stay home, you would.

4. **Your best friend just told you she'll be moving away next month and is really upset about it. You tell her that:**

A. you'll end up writing and talking on the phone even more than you do now! There will be so much more to talk about since you'll be at different schools. And you can always visit. Her move might actually bring you closer!

B. the two of you can keep in touch through Facebook and Twitter. It won't be as good as getting to hang in person every day, but it's the next best thing.

C. you'll stay in contact for a while, but it'll be too hard to keep in touch for long. So you'd better prepare yourselves for the inevitable.

D. you'll probably never see or talk to each other again. People always say they'll keep in touch, but they never actually do. You might as well say your good-byes now.

5. **While riding your bike in the park, you fell and broke your leg—right before your prom! How do you feel?**

A. Actually, you think it's pretty cool. All your friends will want to sign your cast, and making up dances that you can do on crutches might be funny. (All the attention and sympathy you'll get will just be icing on the cake.)

B. Not too bad. It is terrible timing, but you know your friends will help you get around. And if you sit most of the night, no one will even notice that your cast clashes with your dress.

C. It's kind of a bummer. You were really hoping to wear your cute kitten-heeled shoes, but you'll be wearing a huge clunky white cast instead. Still, it could have been worse. You could've broken both legs!

D. It stinks. There's no way you'll have a good time now, so you might as well skip it.

Give yourself 1 point for every time you answered **A**, 2 points for every **B**, 3 points for every **C**, and 4 points for every **D**.

—If you scored between 5 and 12, go to page 179.

—If you scored between 13 and 20, go to page 167.

chapter
FOURTEEN

From Chapter 8: You are as loyal as they come. Even when it's hard (or extremely embarrassing) to stand by your friends and family, you always do, making sure they know you've got their backs. That's probably why you like dogs so much—they stay true-blue to their owners. And the people you care about can trust you to be just as true to them. As long as you aren't pledging your loyalty to the wrong people, it's a great quality to have.

From Chapter 10: Congratulations! You are a born leader. Never one to wait around for someone else to take charge, you prefer to step up to the plate and show others what to do. You would make an excellent CEO, coach, teacher, or entrepreneur. Just be aware that you aren't always the only one who wants to take the reins. Being a good team player is often just as important as being able to lead the way.

Clearly, Jessie has lost her mind. Nothing else could explain her accusing you of lying to her because you're jealous. But Jessie has been your friend since forever, and no way are you letting her crash and burn in front of the whole school just because she's gone temporarily bananas. Somehow you've got to prove to her that what you're saying about Lisa and Maria setting her up to fail is true.

Okay, what you decide to do next is so unlike you, and if there were any other way you would do it. But desperate times call for desperate measures. You take out your Sidekick and text the one person you know could help you, asking her to meet you in the girls' bathroom in the basement. Hardly anyone ever uses that one, so you know you'll have some privacy. She immediately texts back, saying she'll meet you in the bathroom in five.

You get there first, making it down to the basement in record time. And it's no wonder this bathroom doesn't get used very often. It's freezing in there! And it's so out of the way that the janitorial staff seems to pretty much ignore it too. There are cobwebs forming in the corners of the ceiling, and half the stalls are missing toilet paper. If this were a crime novel, you'd be the nervous detective, waiting to meet up with a shifty informant.

Of course, you've never read about an informant that hopes to be on E! one day, telling the world all the latest juicy celebrity gossip. You have been waiting for only a few minutes when the door swings open and Amy Choi walks in.

"Hey!" she says excitedly, her eyes darting around as if she expects flashing cameras or something. "What's going on? You never call to tell me stuff. This must be good!"

"I don't know if 'good' is the word I'd use," you say sullenly, rubbing your arms for warmth. You have broken out in goose bumps everywhere, partially from the draft in the basement and partially because you're remembering the big fight you and Jessie had earlier. You aren't used to not being on speaking terms with your best friend. It doesn't feel good at all. "I need your help, Amy."

Amy nods, as if she gets asked for help all the time and this doesn't surprise her in the least. "Okay," she says, brushing her bangs out of her eyes. "What can I do?"

You take a deep breath. "Well, I overheard Lisa and Maria talking about how they were going to get Jessie to make a fool of herself at the audition today. Only, Jessie doesn't believe me! They're being super nice to her, so she thinks they're her friends and that I'm just jealous. Can you believe that?" You feel yourself getting angry all over again.

But Amy doesn't look outraged at all. She rubs her chin with one delicate hand. "Well . . . are you?" she asks.

"Of course not!" you shout. Your voice bounces off the walls and echoes back to you, sounding less convincing every time. Okay, maybe you are kind of jealous that Jessie had the guts to audition and you didn't. And maybe seeing the cool girls accept Jessie into their clique while completely ignoring you did sting a little bit. But if Lisa and Maria are the kind of friends that come with being popular, you'll stick to being a nobody, thanks.

"Okay, okay," Amy says quickly. "Just checking. So what do you need me to do?"

"I know you have a really good video recorder in your phone." *The better to make embarrassing YouTube videos of your classmates with,* you stop yourself from saying. "If I can get Lisa and Maria to admit what they're up to, can you record it for me?"

"Sure!" Amy answers with zero hesitation. This is right up her alley. "But how are you going to get them to admit anything on video?"

You smile slowly, remembering your little hideout in the auditorium. "Just leave it to me."

After your next class you pace near Maria's and Lisa's lockers. You know they'll come by to drop off the humongous history textbooks they needed for the last period. And this time instead of hiding you plan to confront them.

"How long do I have to sit like this?" Amy complains from the same seat in the auditorium you hid in not too long ago. "My back is cramping and I'm missing out on all the between-classes talk!"

"Shh!" you hiss. "Not too much longer. Here they come!"

You try your best to contain your anger as you spot Maria and Lisa coming toward you, each hugging a heavy textbook to her chest. When Maria sees you leaning against her locker, her dark brown eyes narrow suspiciously. Her straight black hair swings to the left as she leans over to whisper something in Lisa's ear. She looks in your direction suddenly, no doubt wondering what lowly you would have to talk to them about.

"What are you doing in front of my locker?" Maria asks snottily.

"Well, Maria," you speak up, hoping Amy is getting all this, "I just wanted you guys to know that Jessie is my friend, and giving her bad advice so that she'll do lousy at the auditions really stinks."

Lisa gives you an appraising look, seeming to decide that this must be a lucky guess. No way could you know what they had planned. "I have no clue what you're talking about."

Hmm . . . you hadn't banked on them denying everything. Time to switch tactics a bit.

You look them both up and down. "Yeah, I guess you're right. It would be crazy for me to think you two could come up with something that smart. It probably makes your brains hurt just to get out of bed in the morning."

"Hey!" Maria says, getting in your face now. "I'm plenty smart. Your friend is the dumb one for actually being stupid enough to believe she sounds good singing that Taylor Swift song. Once she follows our advice and screeches out that sappy chorus, they'll beg Mona to sing the solo."

Lisa pinches Maria to shut her up, but Maria just says

"Ow!" and keeps on going. "She even thinks we're her BFFs now! As if. She's so gullible."

"Maybe so," you reply. "But at least she has real BFFs to back her up. And when I tell her what you're up to, we'll choose a better song for her and demolish Mona at the auditions!"

"Oh yeah?" Lisa says. "And why would she believe you? It's your word against—"

"Actually," Amy interrupts, popping up from her auditorium hiding place, "it's your word against this video. Say cheese!" She holds up her phone, showing them that she's been videotaping the whole ugly exchange.

The last thing on the video is an image of Maria and Lisa looking into Amy's videophone and turning bright red.

"Sorry we had to show you that," you say to Jessie, handing the phone back to Amy. "But you wouldn't believe me."

Jessie slides down into a seat in the empty auditorium, where you asked her to meet you before the last class of the day. "So . . . none of the girls were being nice to me because they liked me?" Jessie moans.

"Well, I think Shawna and Dionne and some of the others are genuinely nice. They weren't in on this. It was all Lisa and Maria's idea. And they only did it so that Mona would be less of a brat."

"Oh." Knowing why someone was a total jerk to you sometimes doesn't help. Jessie stares down at her hot pink nail polish in disappointment. But then she looks up at you, horror creeping over her face. "Oh God, I was sooo awful to you and you were just trying to help me. I'm sorry! I was acting like we were on *The Hills* or something. So much drama!"

You wave her apology away, acting like it was no big deal. "Please. Don't even worry about it. I knew you'd eventually stop being a total nut job." You smile good-naturedly and playfully push her shoulder.

"Gee, thanks," she says, giving you a gentle shove back. "But now what do I do? If I don't go to the audition, it'll look like they scared me off. But if I do . . ." She trails off, the possibilities being too horrible to mention.

"Don't worry, I have that under control too," you assure Jessie. "Did I mention that I signed up to be a student judge?"

Jessie's eyes bug out of her head. "You did?" You nod. "Oh, you're the best!" she cries and gives you one of her patented Jessie Miller bear hugs.

You spend the next few minutes going over the Miley Cyrus song that you think Jessie will sound much better singing since it's more in her range. She doesn't really have any time to practice, but with a loyal friend like you by her side she's willing to give it her best shot. You know your fellow judges will expect you to vote for Mona just because they are—but unlike some of them, you have a mind of your own.

Finally! You've exposed the mean girls in your midst for the trouble-makers they are, and you have patched things up with your BFF, Jessie. Even Amy Choi's meddlesome ways came in handy for once. Now that you and Jessie are back on track, everything seems right with the world again. But not so fast! You've still got the audition coming up. After finding out that Lisa and Maria were conspiring against her (and hearing what they really thought of her singing), Jessie still has enough guts to hit the stage, this time with a new song that doesn't make her sound like a banshee. It may not be too late to score one for your group of indefinables after all. But will Jessie be able to pull off the upset of a lifetime?

QUIZ TIME!

Sorry, no quiz this time. You and Jessie are fresh out of choices. Nothing left to do but cross your fingers and hope for the best! Head to the auditions on page 208.

chapter
FIFTEEN

From Chapter 8: You must have your reasons, but you're not always the most loyal person on earth. Sometimes it isn't smart to be loyal, especially when it puts you in a bad spot. But if you stick by people when they need you, you might find that they are more loyal to you when you really need them.

From Chapter 10: Your favorite game must be Simon Says, because you like being a follower. Whether that is because you're insecure or you just prefer going with the flow, you go along with the crowd. Being able to follow someone's lead can be a good thing (like on the dance floor or if you're on a rowing crew). But following blindly can get you into trouble. It's fine to be a team player, but try testing out your own leadership skills so that you can see what you're made of.

𝓕𝓻𝓸𝓶 𝓒𝓱𝓪𝓹𝓽𝓮𝓻 *11:* Do you ever get your way? It seems like you always give in to what everyone around you wants. Because you are unwilling, unable, or afraid to speak up, you must end up doing a lot of things you don't want to do. It's classic peer pressure and you aren't the first to fall victim to it. Perhaps you think your friends won't like you as much if you don't give in. But ask yourself this: What kind of friends would pressure you to do anything you don't want to do? If they're your real friends, they won't mind if you say no once in a while so that you can do what's right for you. In fact, they might respect you more for standing up for yourself.

You are sitting at the judges' table in the now-crowded auditorium feeling more uncomfortable than ever. The moment the whole school has been waiting for is finally here: the choir auditions. It seems like every student in the building is crammed into the auditorium like sardines. Even Holly and Mary, the gloom-and-doom duo, are here, sitting right up front. You search the crowd for Jimmy's face, knowing that he would give you a reassuring smile and maybe a goofy thumbs-up, and you would instantly feel better. But then you remember that Jimmy must already be at the community center, dealing with his own stress. You're on your own.

Out of the corner of your eye, you see Jessie waiting for her turn onstage. She is bouncing up and down on one foot and then the other, cracking her neck, like a boxer before a fight. And Lena is right by her side, patting her on the back one minute and then stopping to huddle with Charlie, no doubt about the blog. You are positive that Jessie is trying to make eye contact with you, maybe hoping for a little encouragement. But you just can't bear to face her, especially with Lisa and Maria sitting right next to you being all chummy. You know the only reason they are letting you into their little clique is that they want you to vote for Mona. If only there were a trapdoor beneath the judges' table. You would gladly go sailing through it right about now.

After a few hopeful younger kids audition, all of them getting mediocre reactions from the crowd, Mona Winston makes her way to the stage. She stands confidently behind the mike and announces, "I'll be singing 'Party in the USA' by Miley Cyrus." Then she nods to an older boy sitting at the piano. She came prepared with sheet music and an accompanist? Sheesh. How is anyone supposed to compete with that?

You close your eyes and hope against hope that Mona's singing is as awful as her personality. But as the first few words reach your ears, you have to face the terrible truth: Mona isn't half bad. Actually, she's pretty good. Not mindblowing or anything, but much better than you thought she'd be. After she finishes, the crowd cheers for her like crazy and a few of your fellow judges give her a standing O. You'd like to think most people just liked the song, not necessarily the singer. But you can't deny that Mona did it justice. Annoyingly, she blows a few kisses to the audience before taking a little bow and exiting the stage with a smug grin on her face.

After Mona's audition you have to suffer through Mark's extended version of the *Little Mermaid* classic "Part of Your World." (It's pretty excruciating, but Mark isn't taking his audition too seriously.) The guys from his baseball team do the wave in his honor as Mark leaves the stage triumphantly.

Next up is Lizette singing "One Step at a Time" by Jordin Sparks. Celia and Delia, Lizette's twin cousins, hit the stage with her. (According to Lizette, they insisted that she needed backup dancers and she got tired of arguing with them.) It's actually a pretty cute performance. That is, until Celia accidentally steps on Delia's foot and they start bickering onstage, forcing Lizette to stop singing just as she's hitting the big notes at the end. "One step at a tiiiii —" she begins, cutting herself off abruptly to drag her ever-embarrassing cousins off the stage, one twin at a time. Once they're off she grabs each one by an ear and escorts them out of the auditorium, muttering angrily the whole way. The audience can't help laughing and neither can you. That whole episode really helped break the tension in the room.

Finally it is Jessie's turn. You feel pretty good about the fact that she is following that disastrous incident. Maybe she won't sound so bad after that. But when Jessie gets to the middle of "You Belong with Me," the sound is just as bad as you expected — a fact she seems blissfully unaware of. As she belts out the chorus — "Why can't you seeee-eee-heee, you belong with meeee-eeeee-eeeee-eee?" — you actually hear groans from the crowd, and you see a few of the cheerleaders plugging their ears. Thankfully, Jessie's eyes are squeezed shut almost the whole time. When she finally finishes the song and opens her eyes, Lisa and Maria each give Jessie a big fake thumbs-up while secretly bumping fists behind the chairs. Jessie smiles radiantly, her blond ponytail bouncing with glee.

Meanwhile, you are in friendship hell. You're not sure who you are more furious with: the girls sitting next to you at the judges' table for tricking Jessie into going with a song that makes her usually melodic voice sound like screaming monkeys, or yourself for not telling your BFF the truth and sparing her this lesson in mortification. As much as you hate the popular girls in this moment, Jessie is your friend, so the blame falls right on your already-sagging shoulders.

After Jessie leaves the stage and takes a seat next to Charlie and Lena, Jasmine Viera tentatively makes her way to the mike. Since she's a little shorter than Jess, she has to pull it down to her level.

"All right, Ms. Viera," Mr. Parker says into his own microphone. "Whenever you're ready."

Jasmine gives a quick nod, clears her throat, and then starts belting out "Apologize" by One Republic. The previously noisy room suddenly quiets down so much you could hear a pin drop. Jasmine's voice rocks! As she sings, "It's too late to apologiiiize. It's too laaaaaate," she hits all the high notes effortlessly and emphasizes all the right words. She's actually better than Mona and Jessie put together! It's pretty obvious who should win.

But just when you're thinking about casting your vote for Jasmine, Lisa pointedly slides her ballot in front of you. Under "Soloists," she has checked the box next to Mona's name. When you look from the ballot to Lisa's freckled face and bright red hair, she leans over and whispers, "Remember: Voting for Mona is the key to a whole new social life. Think about it."

If the voting were done by secret ballot, you wouldn't care what Lisa said. But Mr. Parker already explained that he'll go around and ask everyone for their vote—meaning that everyone will know who you choose.

Mr. Parker gives all the judges a few minutes to make their selections. You agonize over your choices. You could vote for Jessie, but you would be the only one. And even though Jasmine deserves your vote, what would be the point of going against the other student judges? Jessie still wouldn't win and you'd just make enemies out of Maria and Lisa. (Not to mention Mona, who already hates your guts.)

First Mr. Parker announces the lucky kids who will get to be in the choir. Lizette made it in, despite her audition fiasco, as did Kevin Minks, Melanie Sawyer, Sanjay Hirash, and a bunch of younger kids you don't know very well. Then the faculty judges reveal their votes for star soloist. Some of them vote for Mona, but most vote for Jasmine. Then it's the students' turn. Surprisingly, Shawna and Dionne both vote for Jasmine, causing a stir around the room. But Adam, Lisa, and Maria all vote for Mona, bringing the score to a tie. And guess who gets the tie-breaker vote? Got a mirror handy? Because you guessed it: It's you.

You glance over at Jessie and see Lena squeezing her hand. Jessie looks close to tears. Everyone in the room seems to be holding their breath. You can't put it off any longer.

You hold up your ballot and announce, "I voted for Mona."

Immediately the silence is broken and kids everywhere start congratulating one another, or consoling the ones who didn't make it (like Mark). As you scan the auditorium, you happen to lock eyes with Lena, whose disappointment in you is written all over her face. Shawna and Dionne seem pretty distant all of a sudden too. You aren't sure what feels worse: letting all of them down, or letting yourself down.

Yikes. Everything about that audition process was harsh. Listening to Mark Bukowski butcher a Disney classic? Painful. Failing to warn Jessie that she was about to humiliate herself in front of the whole school? Heinous. And finally, casting your vote for Mona instead of Jasmine or Jessie just because you want to stay on Planet Popular? Brutal. The worst part is that all this could have been avoided if you had not given up on your own singing dream quite so quickly. Oh well. You can't change anything you've done today. But unlike what One Republic thinks, it's never too late to apologize.

QUIZ TIME!

Didn't you read the last line above? Go to page 161 and apologize to your friends, pronto!

chapter
SIXTEEN

No matter how hard you try, you're bound to make some mistakes. Not that you need anyone to tell you that—you made a ton of mistakes today! You haven't been the best friend you could be, and let's face it—the lure of popularity steered you away from who you really are. Or at least who you hope to be. The beauty of making mistakes, though, is that you can learn from them and try to do better next time. And if you have really good friends, once you apologize they might just forgive you.

You know exactly where to find Jessie: the girls' bathroom on the basement level of the school. You both know that no one ever comes down here because it's so out of the way. Plus this bathroom is always freezing. For those reasons, it is the perfect place to come when you need to cry but don't want anyone to walk in on you doing it.

Walking in on Jessie will be one more thing you have to apologize for, but what's one more "sorry" when you already owe Jessie a million of them? You swing open the door and sure enough, there she is, sitting on the oversize counter next to the sinks sobbing into her hands. It has been ages since you've seen Jess cry like this (the last time being when she accidentally threw out her Justin Bieber concert tickets and couldn't go see the show), and you feel pretty crummy for being the cause of her tears now.

"Hey, Jessie," you say hesitantly, still holding the door open. "Mind if I come in?"

Jessie doesn't remove her hands from her face. Instead she lifts them along with her head and peers at you through her spread fingers, the way you would peek at a horror movie. You can't blame her. You have been kind of scary today.

"It's a free country," she says finally, turning away from you so that you can see only her profile. Her button nose and bony chin seem so delicate. And the brightly colored hoop earrings dangling from her ears look way too happy to be worn by a person who is crying this hard.

You let the door swing shut behind you as you edge closer to the window, rubbing your arms for warmth. Seriously, is the principal storing frozen food down here or what? You sit down on the windowsill next to your BFF, talking to her back.

"Look, Jessie, I'm sooo sorry about the way I acted. I was a jerk."

"A huge jerk," Jessie corrects you tearfully.

"Yeah, a huge jerk."

"You really embarrassed me."

"I know."

"In front of everyone!"

"I *know*."

"Why did you do it?"

"I don't know."

"So far I'm not too impressed with this apology," Jessie says, dabbing at her eyes with a wad of tissues.

She's right. You're totally blowing this. Time to dig deep.

"Well, see, it's like this," you begin, searching for the right words. "I think . . . I just got so caught up in the clique stuff that I went a little cuckoo." Even though Jessie isn't looking at you, you make the universal sign for "crazy" by whirling your index finger in a circle next to your temple. "I guess this social-status stuff matters more to me than I thought," you admit sheepishly. "Try saying that three times fast."

"Social-status stuff, social-status stuff, social-slatus shtuff . . . ," Jessie attempts immediately. "Dang! Almost had it." You giggle. It's like she's forgotten for a moment that she's mad at you. But once she remembers, she grows quiet again.

"Anyway, I know I made all the wrong moves today. But you and Lena mean the world to me and I would never do anything to hurt you — at least not on purpose. You know that, right?"

Jessie finally looks at you through puffy blue eyes. She nods. "I know."

"Good," you answer, relief washing over you. For a minute there you thought you were going to lose her. "I'm really, really sorry, Jess. Because you and Lena are my best friends in the whole world and I'm just really, really, really sor—"

"All right! All right! I get it!" Jessie interrupts you. "You're sorry. Stop being such a sap." She gives you a sarcastic eye roll accompanied by a half smile so that you know she's kidding. Then, looking serious again, she says, "I'm sorry too. I know it was my idea to go after the cliques in the first place, but I got sucked in as much as you did." Jessie bites her lip. "Remember back in second grade when all of us were friends and the only thing you needed to be cool was a really big box of crayons?"

You smile at the memory. It's true. Back then any kid with a box of sixty-four Crayolas and a crayon sharpener was a superstar. "Definitely."

"I miss that."

"Me too," you tell Jessie. "But at least we'll always be friends. And we can pinkie-swear on that." You hold out your pinkie just like you used to do in second grade. Jessie reaches out her pinkie and gives yours a good shake. And little by little, things between you start to go back to normal.

"Sooo . . . do you wanna go to the auditorium?" you ask.

"Negative," Jessie answers, making a giant X with her arms. "The auditions are over now anyway."

"True." That means no Carnegie Hall for either one of you. Nice going. "Did I mention how sorry I am?" you repeat for the millionth time.

Jessie balls up her fist and shakes it at you. "If you apologize to me one more time . . ."

"Okay, okay." You giggle. "No need to get violent."

"Hey, I know where we could go to cheer ourselves up," Jessie says with a devilish grin.

"Great. I'll go anywhere to get out of this ice-cold bathroom! What did you have in mind?"

"Well, I'll give you a hint: There will be lots of stuff on the walls, it'll smell like paint, and a certain comic-book geek with butterfingers will be there."

OMG! She's talking about Jimmy's art exhibit. So much has happened today, you almost forgot! In a flash you grab Jessie's hand and pull her out of the bathroom. *"Let's go!"*

Good girl. You owned up to your bad behavior and made amends with your bestie. You did manage to wreck the plan to overrule the power cliques. And you both missed out on your chance to set the music world on fire, but who needs props, fame, and fortune when you've got each other? Okay, okay, fame and fortune might have been nice, but if it's meant to be, there will be plenty of other opportunities. For now you're more than happy to hang with your real friends . . . and support your favorite artist.

QUIZ TIME!

Come on, you don't really need a quiz to tell you where you should go next, do you? Get over to page 193 and prepare to be blown away!

chapter
SEVENTEEN

Your glass is definitely half empty. It's great that you are realistic enough to know that bad things happen sometimes. After all, if you are prepared for the bumps and bruises of the world, they won't come as such a shock. The problem is that you seem to always think the worst. And whether you realize it or not, walking around with a storm cloud over your head only serves to block the sun. Try looking on the bright side now and then. If you expect good things to happen, they just might.

"Don't make me drag you in there," Jessie threatens, both of her fists on her hips. "You know I'll do it." You look over at Lena but find no help there either.

"Don't look at me," Lena says evenly. "I'm with Jessie. If

you don't audition, you're going to ruin our blog's big finale."

Charlie leans in sympathetically. "I'd let you off the hook,
but the story is really good so far, if I do say so myself." He
and Lena nod at each other and shake hands like lifelong
business partners.

"And helllooo," Jessie insists. "There's the little matter of
getting to go to New York City and sing in Carnegie Hall!
Do you have any idea how many celebrities are walking
around all over the place there?" Jessie throws up her
hands in frustration and paces up and down the hallway. "I
actually convinced kids who are usually too shy to *speak* let
alone sing to come audition, but you won't? Jeez, even *I'm*
gonna do it and I don't have an amazing voice like yours. I
just can't believe you're giving up without bothering to
try!"

You have been sitting on the floor next to the row of lockers just outside the auditorium, your arms wrapped around
your knees, while Jessie, Lena, and Charlie stand over you
looking like giants. You know how much they want you to
go in there, but it's like they didn't hear you when you told
them the situation.

"Guys, did you forget about Lizette's text already? Mona
stole my song! And she's going on before me so I'll look like
an idiot if I sing the same thing she did. Plus half her
friends are judges. I don't have a chance! I'm not going
through with it, all right?" You know that you're whining.

But you can't help it. You had such high hopes this morning. It figures that everything would go wrong.

Before Jessie has a chance to lay into you any more, Jasmine Viera comes speeding down the hall toward the auditorium, her long black hair flying out behind her. You can hear her humming a scale in C major. Her forehead is covered in a thin sheen of sweat and she keeps biting her bottom lip. Know-it-all Jasmine is always so pulled together and totally in control—sweating and biting her lip is not like her. If you didn't know any better, you'd say she was scared.

"Hey, Jas," Charlie calls to her just as she is reaching for the auditorium door. (Charlie and Jasmine have been friends since the summer, when they both tried and failed to win tickets to Shawna's birthday party. Being a fellow overachiever, Charlie is one of the few who is allowed to call her Jas.) "Are you going in there?"

Jasmine glances down at her hand on the doorknob, then back at Charlie. *Duh,* her look says.

Jessie rolls her eyes. "He means . . . are you going in there to audition?"

"That's the idea." Jasmine peeks into the crowded auditorium and sees the long table of judges. "Yep, that's the scary, nerve-wracking idea. . . ."

"See?" Jessie whirls around to face you again, standing between you and Jasmine. "She's scared, but she's still going in."

Jasmine leans over to peek around Jessie. "You're auditioning too?"

You open your mouth to answer but Lena's voice comes out instead. "She *was*."

"But now she's backing out because she's afraid to compete with Mona," Jessie finishes, shaking her head.

"I am not!" you say before Charlie has a chance to add his two cents. "I just don't see the point of entering a standoff with Mona if I'm only going to lose, all right?"

You figure Jasmine, at least, will understand. She hates to lose too. Without even taking her hand off the doorknob, Jasmine straightens her back. *She's about to let them have it,* you think. She'll come to your defense.

"Your attitude stinks," Jasmine says, looking directly at . . . you! Okay, not quite the defense you were hoping for.

"Huh?"

"You heard me." Jasmine takes another peek into the auditorium, then turns back to you. "I don't know if I can beat Mona either—and I really don't want to face all of *them*." She points a thumb over her shoulder at the gathering crowd. "But at least *I'm* willing to go for it."

"Easy for you to say," you gripe. "You're so used to winning everything."

"Not everything," Jasmine says pointedly. You know she's probably thinking of when she blew the question that would have scored her a ticket to Shawna's party. "And anyway, the reason I win so often is that I *try* more often. I don't always come out on top; I just think I will."

Huh. Maybe Jasmine really does know it all. You have absolutely no comeback for what she said.

"Anyway," she goes on, suddenly looking bored with the loser vibe you've got going on in the hall, "I've gotta get in there. I think I'm up next." She swings open the door and marches toward her doom. She must be nuts.

"See?" Jessie says, gesturing toward the door Jasmine just disappeared through. "She's not gonna let mean ol' Mona scare her away."

You shrug your shoulders miserably. You know your friends are right, but you're still unable to face the stage. "It's her funeral."

Jessie throws up her hands again in disgust. "*Ugh!* I've had it! Come on, guys," she says, motioning Lena and Charlie inside. "*Some* of us have to get ready to sing."

It doesn't take long for you to realize that even if you don't plan to audition, you should at least go in and support Jessie. Especially since she only signed up so that you wouldn't have to go through it alone.

You sneak into the back of the auditorium and spot two empty seats next to Lena and Charlie. One is obviously for Jessie, who is hovering near the stage awaiting her turn. But they saved a seat for you too, in case you changed your mind. Nice. Even when you've had a fight (usually because you're being a bonehead), your friends are still there for you. The sight of the saved seat makes you feel extra bad for letting them down. You slip into it and see they both have their BlackBerrys on their laps, trying to figure out the ending for today's blog. Jasmine is just finishing up. She's singing "Apologize" by One Republic and she sounds really amazing. When she sings the last note, everyone starts clapping wildly—popular kids and nerds alike.

It's a tough act to follow, but Jessie hits the stage next. You realize you haven't even asked her what she'll be singing, you were so wrapped up in your own freak-out. You are pleasantly surprised when Jess breaks into that Jason Mraz song "I'm Yours." She doesn't have the greatest voice on earth, but it doesn't even matter. The song is so cute and Jessie is dancing around the stage, clearly having fun. Before long, the whole audience is singing along with her and rocking from side to side. By the time she gets to the last line, her single voice has turned into a hundred. Again, the place erupts in cheers.

You catch Mona giving her friends a dirty look, and they stop clapping immediately, as if they've been caught doing something wrong. She is still staring them down as she makes her way to the stage. But as soon as her hand touches the mike, she breaks into a radiant (and superfake) smile.

"Name and song choice," Mr. Parker says formally into his own microphone.

"Mona Winston, and I'll be singing 'You Belong with Me' by Taylor Swift."

She scans the crowd before she starts singing, and when she notices you her smile grows even wider. Then she winks at you. She actually winks! Infuriating.

"That little troll," Jessie says bitterly, having slipped into her seat next to yours following her big success. "She has some nerve."

You can only nod in agreement since you're too angry to speak. The worst part is, Mona wasn't all talk either. She's not half bad. Not as good as you might have been, and not as good as Jasmine, but not bad.

Lena rests a comforting hand over yours and looks at you with sincere brown eyes. "Hey, I know you think the odds are stacked against you, but are you sure you don't want to give it a shot? I think you might regret it if you don't at least try."

"Yeah," Jessie says, squeezing your left shoulder, her voice no longer bearing a hint of anger. "Besides, I know you would blow the judges away. And even if you don't, who cares? It would still mean you stood up to Mona, and how good would that feel?"

"Dang it, you guys," you start, looking from one to the other. "I just hate it when you make sense." You all smile at one another, and they each take turns hugging you.

When Mr. Parker clears his throat and says into the microphone, "Oh, wait . . . according to my list we have one more person who would like to audition, correct?" He scans the audience before finally resting his eyes on you.

Gulp. Here goes nothing. You stand with your knees shaking like crazy. "I would."

Mona looks appalled. It's so on!

Today has been absolutely crazy so far. For the first time ever, you were sent to the principal's office. You had your phone taken away. You were forced to grovel to Ms. Krell to get it back. You had your song choice stolen. And you got into a fight with your two BFFs after you single-handedly foiled Jessie's plan to topple the power cliques and ruined Lena's blog. And that's in addition to giving up on your rock-star dreams. What did all these negative events have in common (besides you)? Mona Winston. You hate to admit it, but she totally got to you and had you thinking there was no way you could win, so you might as well not even try. Thank goodness your friends care enough to rally around you and encourage you to give it a shot, even though victory is uncertain—to put it mildly. But now that you've finally come around, can you control your anger at Mona long enough to knock the audition out of the park? Only the quiz knows.

QUIZ TIME!

Circle your answers and tally up the points at the end.

1. **When you were really little and your folks refused to buy you some toy you wanted in the store, you would:**
   A. kick and scream and cry until your face was all red and blotchy. Hey, how else were you supposed to react? You really wanted that toy!

B. pout and refuse to speak to your mom for the rest of the day. Throwing a tantrum would have only gotten you into trouble. But the silent treatment definitely let your mom know you were ticked off.

C. beg and beg until your dad would get really annoyed. Eventually you'd give up and do your best to forget about the toy. (It must have worked, since you can't remember now what toy you wanted that long ago!)

D. accept it and play with the toys you already had. You were momentarily disappointed, but not getting a new toy is really no big deal.

2. **You just got your English paper back and the teacher gave you a C-minus. You are:**

A. *outraged!* How could she give you a C-minus? You worked so hard on that paper! As soon as you see the grade, you tear the paper to shreds and storm out of the classroom. Take that!

B. pretty mad. You really thought that was quality work. But since jumping down your teacher's throat will land you in the principal's office, you settle for going on an angry tirade about it in your blog. You've gotta let your irritation out somewhere!

C. disappointed. It seems the teacher didn't quite get where you were coming from. You vow to talk to her about it after class and find out what you can do better next time.

D. concerned. If you thought you deserved an A on that paper, maybe you didn't understand the work as well as you thought. You'll sign up for an English tutor ASAP.

3. **Your best friend knows all about your secret crush on her brother Paul. When she accidentally spills the beans in front of him one day, you:**

A. scream at her for five minutes straight and tell her your friendship is donezo! How could she do that to you?

B. are extremely annoyed. Now you'll never be able to face Paul again! You leave without a word. But you'll hash it out with your friend later. If she ever wants you to confide in her again, she'll have to learn to keep her big mouth shut!

C. are a little upset and spend a day not speaking to your pal. You know it was an accident, and she would never do anything to hurt you on purpose. But you need some time to cool down.

D. are embarrassed. You guess your secret is out! You're sure your friend didn't mean to let it slip. So the only real question is: Does Paul like you back?

4. **Even though you've told her not to a gazillion times, your sister wore your favorite white sweater to her friend's pizza party and now there's a huge marinara-sauce stain right on the front. What do you do when she confesses?**

A. March into her room and destroy her favorite music box.

An eye for an eye! That might seem harsh, but you warned her not to take your stuff and she did it anyway—now it's payback time!

B. Tell your parents what she did and let them hand out her punishment, then spend the rest of the day locked in your room so that your sis can't get in. You wouldn't normally snitch, but you're sick of her ruining your stuff.

C. You freak out for a while. (That was the best sweater ever, and now it smells like spaghetti!) You're mad at your sister for a long time but eventually just let it go. She's family after all, even if she does sometimes get on your nerves.

D. You tell her it's okay. Yes, you did love that sweater. But your sister's apology is sincere, and she's way more important to you than any piece of clothing. To teach her to respect your things, though, she'll have to make your bed for a week.

5. **Your status updates on Facebook tend to be all about:**

A. whatever made you angry that day. Most things get a rise out of you, so there's no end to the number of things you can rage about!

B. little things that annoy you. It seems like every time your day is going well, something happens to ruin it—you get a tear in your tights, your teacher springs a pop quiz on you, you step in gum. . . . Sometimes it's hard to keep your cool.

C. whatever happened to you in the past few hours, good or bad. Some days are pretty crummy, but some days are awesome. Your Facebook family is a part of all your ups and downs.

D. anything positive that's happened that day. You can usually even make a joke about bad stuff too. (It was pretty hilarious when you fell on your butt while you were ice-skating.)

Give yourself 1 point for every time you answered **A**, 2 points for every **B**, 3 points for every **C**, and 4 points for every **D**.

   —If you scored between 5 and 12, go to page 188.
   —If you scored between 13 and 20, go to page 179.

chapter EIGHTEEN

From Chapters 12 or 13: Your side of the street is always sunny—even in the shade! When your friends are feeling down, you can usually cheer them up, since you have the uncanny ability to look on the bright side. And because you expect great things to happen, you aren't surprised when they do. Having such a positive attitude is awesome. Make sure you aren't always viewing the world through rose-colored glasses, though. Life can be tough and sometimes the worst-case scenarios come true. But since you're such an optimist, dealing with the occasional downer is a breeze: You know that things can always change for the better.

From Chapter 17: Congratulations! When you get upset, you know how to keep it in check. In fact, you're so even-tempered that your loved ones sometimes think you're a saint! Hardly anything gets you riled and you can always come up with a better way to handle an aggravating situation than to throw a tantrum or resort to violence. One word of caution: If you really are boiling over inside and simply not letting it out, you might explode one day and it won't be pretty. As long as you express your emotions—whatever they might be—in a healthy way, you'll be just fine.

After the little pep talk from your friends, you stroll up to the stage fully believing you can do this and that you're going to do a great job. You can't lie; it did bother you to hear Mona sing the song you were planning to use. (Even though Mona's deviance isn't too surprising, you're amazed that she would sink so low.) You could waste time being angry with Mona, but you'd rather take her attempt at sabotage as an enormous confidence booster. After all, she wouldn't feel the need to do something so underhanded if she didn't consider you a legitimate threat, right? Right.

There is one teensy problem, though: What are you gonna sing? Mona's plan, while evil, was also genius. Stealing your song has thrown you off your game a little. But you refuse to let her get to you. You'll just have to move on to plan B.

Since Jessie did so much to be your moral support today—even going so far as to audition in order to keep you company—you figure a great way to repay her would be to sing a song you know she'll love.

"Name and song choice, please," Mr. Parker says from the judges' table.

You state your name and then look directly at Jessie when you say, "I'll be singing 'The Climb' by Miley Cyrus."

Jessie's face automatically lights up. You know that she's a huge Miley fan, and "The Climb" is one of her all-time favorite songs. Lena smiles at you and then furiously taps away at her BlackBerry. Not only have you made Jessie's day with your song choice, but you're about to give Lena and Charlie the perfect ending for their blog.

You start singing, soft and tentative at first. But eventually the lyrics carry you away and you put your heart and soul into each word. You are barely aware of the judges as your voice soars out over the crowd. What surprises you more than anything is how completely natural it feels to be up there, commanding everyone's attention. You could get used to this! As you build up to the big finale, you raise your left arm to the sky, close your eyes, and belt out, "It's the cliiiiiiiiiiiiiiimb!" You hold the note for what seems like an eternity.

When you finally finish, there is a second of stunned silence, followed by the loudest applause you've ever heard in your life. Everyone's jaws are on the floor—including Mona's. Ahh, success tastes so sweet!

On your way back to your seat, everybody you pass gives you a high five or a pat on the back. You might as well be on MTV, because you definitely feel like a rock star right now.

You still have to get past the judges, though. You may have just killed the audition, but Mona's friends are on the panel.

As Mr. Parker asks them to reveal their votes for soloist one by one, you get the biggest shock of all. Although there are a couple of holdouts who insist on voting for Mona, you win by a landslide. The soloist spot is yours!

"I just knew you would blow everybody away!" Jessie gushes. "Didn't I tell you? Look out, Taylor Swift, there's a new diva in town!"

Jessie gives you another bear hug as you try to maintain your balance in the middle of the crowd of kids surrounding you. This must be what Robert Pattinson feels like when he's being swarmed by fans. You wouldn't want to deal with that everywhere you went, but right now it feels pretty good. Mona and a few of her friends are still shooting you death glares, but you don't even care.

Right behind Jessie, Charlie and Lena are waiting to congratulate you too. "That was quite impressive, young lady," Lena says in her grown-up voice. "Thank goodness you decided to audition! We couldn't have made up a better ending for the blog. Let me be the first to congratulate you on striking a blow for indefinables everywhere!"

Charlie nods his agreement as he straightens his tie. "Not bad at all," he says. "We might have to make your rise to stardom a regular feature."

Jasmine, standing just behind Lena, reaches between her and Charlie to shake your hand. "Great job," Jasmine says. "I can't wait to be in the choir with you."

"Thanks, Jasmine!" you say sincerely. "You were great too. Carnegie Hall, here we come!"

"Uh, excuse me, but before you go running off to New York, how 'bout letting me take you out to celebrate?" It's Joey Cruz, from the library, looking so much like a young Derek Jeter it's scary.

You never really expected him to speak to you again after you met in the library. But just when you thought you'd completely blown your chances of ever being accepted by the popular crowd, here comes Joey, asking you out! It's too good to be true. "Are you serious?" you utter, completely surprised.

"Sure! After that performance, and of course all your hard work in the library, it's the least I can do. So what do you say?"

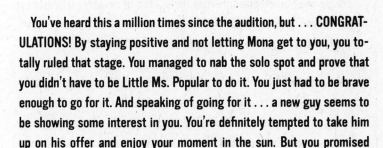

You've heard this a million times since the audition, but . . . CONGRAT-ULATIONS! By staying positive and not letting Mona get to you, you to-tally ruled that stage. You managed to nab the solo spot and prove that you didn't have to be Little Ms. Popular to do it. You just had to be brave enough to go for it. And speaking of going for it . . . a new guy seems to be showing some interest in you. You're definitely tempted to take him up on his offer and enjoy your moment in the sun. But you promised Jimmy you would go to his art exhibit to be there for *his* moment in the sun, remember? So do you go support your longtime crush and good friend Jimmy, or do you opt to get to know someone new? Still torn? Maybe the quiz will help you decide.

QUIZ TIME!

Circle your answers and tally up the points at the end.

1. **You scored straight As on your report card! As a reward, your parents offer to take you out to dinner anywhere you want, and you can order whatever you want too. What do you go with?**

   A. Your favorite restaurant, where you can order your favorite meal. Why get anything else when you know for sure that you'll love what you always get?

   B. Your favorite restaurant. But this time you'll order a different dessert. (This is a special occasion, after all.)

   C. You let your parents pick the restaurant. They know what you like so you're sure they'll pick something great. (At least you hope!)

   D. You hop on the Internet, find a list of nearby restaurants, and pick one you've never even heard of. Eating somewhere you've never been before can be exciting!

2. **You and your friends are heading to the beach. What do you wear?**

   A. The same trusty blue bathing suit and matching flip-flops you always wear. You don't see the point of trying to keep up with trends that change every season.

   B. Your usual blue one-piece suit, but this time you'll pair it with the stylin' black sunglasses you just picked up at the mall.

C. You try out a new crocheted tankini you found online, but hang on to your trusty flip-flops. Your friends think it is seriously time for new footwear, but they're just so comfy!

D. You rock a whole new outfit: bright red tank set, espadrilles, and a big floppy sun hat. New year, new look!

3. **What is your iPod MO?**

A. You tend to listen to the same set of songs over and over again, very rarely adding anything new to your list. Who needs new tunes when the classics are so great?

B. You might skip around a little later, but starting with your top ten favorites is a must! (Britney never disappoints.)

C. You put your iPod on shuffle and listen to whatever pops up. You like not knowing what you're going to hear next.

D. Truthfully, you barely even listen to the stuff you just downloaded a week ago. You're way too busy seeking out the latest releases to add to your collection.

4. **Your teacher wants to know what project you'll be entering in this year's science fair. What'll it be?**

A. The erupting volcano. Yes, you've built one two years running, but you know exactly how to do it, and when the fake lava comes pouring out, it's always a real crowd-pleaser.

B. You'll do the photosynthesis experiment at least one kid does every year. Your teachers have seen that one a million times, but it's a surefire A.

C. You saw an experiment on the Discovery Channel that you're dying to try. You'll just have to do an early run-through to make sure you can pull it off.

D. You have no idea! But you confidently tell your teacher that you're going to build a robot. No, you don't know how, but you'll figure it out through trial and error. That's what real scientists do. Plus, when it's all over you'll have a robot butler—awesome!

5. **Your sister has the chicken pox and is stuck in the house for two weeks! And your parents say it's your responsibility to keep her entertained. Tonight she wants to watch a DVD. What do you put on?**

A. *Twilight.* Again. You've both seen it enough times to repeat the dialogue word for word along with the actors. But watching RPatz be all broody and dark never gets old.

B. First *Twilight* (naturally), and then season 1 of *So You Think You Can Dance.* That is one of your sister's favorite shows, but you know she missed an episode or two.

C. You order up some new releases from Netflix. Anything your sis hasn't seen already will do, as long as there's popcorn!

D. Actually, you have a better idea. You pull out your parents' camcorder and decide to make a home video instead. You and your sister can record all the crazy things

you do to pass the time during her chicken pox outbreak,
then watch it later and laugh your heads off.

Give yourself 1 point for every time you answered *A*, 2 points for every *B*,
3 points for every *C*, and 4 points for every *D*.
—If you scored between 5 and 12, go to page 193.
—If you scored between 13 and 20, go to page 198.

chapter NINETEEN

From Chapter 12: Try as you might, you just can't stop thinking negatively. Like Murphy's Law says, if something can go wrong it will. And you believe that if you expect the worst, then anything else comes as a pleasant surprise. But is that really the way you want to live? You don't have to be a little ball of sunshine (especially if that's not how you honestly feel), but focusing on the good things in your life could bring more good things your way.

From Chapter 17: Cool down, hothead! It doesn't take you long at all to reach your boiling point. There are plenty of things during the day that are aggravating (the bus taking off without you, being teased by a bully at school, your parents punishing you for something your little brother did), but flying off the handle won't get you anywhere. If you take a deep breath and count to ten, you'll probably think of a healthier way to deal with all the things that get you riled up than throwing a fit.

Crazy as this is, you are going through with the audition. Jasmine went already, and she sounded awesome. And Jessie auditioned just for fun and seemed to enjoy it, but she wasn't taking it too seriously. You, on the other hand, feel like you're about to face a firing squad.

You just can't help reliving Mona's audition in your head—particularly the moment when she announced she would be singing your song. *My name is Mona Winston, and I'll be singing "You Belong with Me" by Taylor Swift.* Un. Real. And then she didn't even have the common decency to sound horrible. The nerve of that girl!

As you nervously step onto the stage, you try to focus on the fact that all your friends are here to support you. You have a bad feeling about this, but with Lena and Jessie behind you, maybe you'll do all right. You take a deep breath and feel a moment of hope. But then you remember that you haven't come up with a different song to sing. Would you look like the biggest lame-o in the world if you just ran screaming from the auditorium? Yeah, probably. No choice now but to go through with it. You could kill Mona! Your hands start shaking, but you can't tell if it's from nerves or pure rage.

"Name and song selection, please." Mr. Parker looks at you expectantly.

This is going to be humiliating. You mumble your name, and then in the most miserable whisper possible you force yourself to say, "I'll be singing 'You Belong with Me' too."

Ugh. You grab the mike and bring it too close to your mouth, causing a whine of feedback. You hear a couple of giggles in the crowd. You don't blame them. If you were them you would laugh at you too.

At last you start to sing, but your heart just isn't in it. Even though it's the same tune Mona just sang, it sounds completely different—and not in a good way. You're practically whispering the parts you're supposed to belt out. And while Mona used the whole stage, flirting with boys in the audience as she sang the chorus, you are stiff as a board, refusing to move around the stage at all. You might as well be a mannequin. And forget about making eye contact with anyone. You are looking directly at your beat-up sneakers as if they are your only friends in the world.

When the torture finally ends, there is a smattering of confused applause, probably out of pity. Mr. Parker clears his throat and says, "Um, okay. That was an . . . interesting interpretation of the song. Thank you."

Ouch. Everybody knows that when Mr. Parker says "interesting" it's the kiss of death. You hold back your tears as you head to your seat next to Lena. You may be completely mortified, but you still have your pride (whatever scraps of it are left anyway).

"There—are you happy now?" you whisper angrily to Jessie.

"Yes," she answers immediately, to your surprise. "I mean, okay, you weren't exactly Taylor Swift up there, but at least you did it!"

190

"Yeah," Lena agrees. "We're still really proud of you."

"Thanks," you mumble.

When it comes time to reveal the judges' decisions, no one is very surprised. Although Jasmine gave her a run for her money, Mona gets the solo. Annoyingly, she runs back up onstage and starts making an acceptance speech. "I just want to thank everyone who encouraged me and supported my dream. Thanks to Eli, on piano; my friends, for believing in me . . ."

You have to tune out the rest before you turn into the Incredible Hulk and start smashing up the stage. "Can we get out of here now?" you beg your friends.

"Definitely," Jessie says. "I know just the place!" She shares another one of those knowing looks with Lena, who simply nods, hooks her arm around yours, and says, "Let's go."

That was, perhaps, not your best moment. Okay, there's no "perhaps" about it. You tanked, and the whole school was there to see it. (Except Jimmy, thank goodness. You really would have been horrified if he'd witnessed your epic audition fail.) And Mona, who is worse than any comic-book villain, now has even more reason to gloat. Thanks to your inability to conquer your anger and nerves, the solo spot is hers. Thank goodness your friends are there to pick you up off the floor. Even though your audition didn't go as well as you'd hoped (even Mark's was better!), Jessie and Lena are still proud of you for trying. Your BFFs swear they know the perfect thing to pull you out of your funk. Let's hope so, because your only other alternative is locking yourself in your room and never ever coming out.

QUIZ TIME!

Sorry, no quiz this time. You're much too stressed for that. Just trust Lena and Jessie to take you somewhere that will cheer you up. Head over to page 193 and put this whole ugly mess behind you.

chapter
TWENTY

From Chapter 18: You're a creature of habit and you don't like switching up your routine too much. Some people might find that a little ho-hum, but you don't see what's wrong with sticking to what you know. Everything in your life—from your music to your friends to your clothes—is tried and true, and you prefer to keep it that way. It's great that you've found some things that you love (like your trusty flip-flops), but weren't all those things new to you at some point too? Why not branch out a little and try at least one new thing a month? Take a different path home from school, eat a flavor of ice cream you've never tried before, make a new friend. You may not like everything you try, but you might stumble across a few new things that could become old favorites.

From Chapters 16, 18, 19, 21, 23, and 24: Prepare to be wowed!

193

As you walk into the community center, you are amazed by how it has transformed. They have cleared out all the wooden benches and plastic folding chairs, and in their place are art pieces from people in the community. On one podium in the middle of the room is a sculpture of a horse. Beneath is a small plaque that reads:

Horse
Artist: Ida Bukowski
82 years young

Hey! You're pretty sure that's Mark's grandmother. All the pieces are labeled that way, with the title of the work, the name of the artist, and their age, if they choose to provide it. There's some cheese and crackers to munch on, which is great because all of today's drama has left you starving. You just hope they have enough cheese back there to feed an army, because this place is packed!

You turn one corner, Jessie and Lena right behind you, and finally spot what you came to see. The entire back wall is devoted to your favorite artist: Jimmy Morehouse. And the artist himself has spotted you too. When he does, he stops shifting nervously from one foot to the other, a huge smile spreads across his face, and his big green eyes light up. He has managed to get most of the paint out of his hair, which is now brushed back in careful waves, and instead of the ratty button-down shirt, he is wearing a corduroy blazer.

It is the sharpest you've ever seen him look. This show must be serious business!

When Lena notices that you've made eye contact with Jimmy, she yanks Jessie's arm back and says, "Hey, Jessie, isn't this a fascinating sculpture? I think it's made out of recycled soda cans!"

"Wow!" Jessie exclaims, catching on quickly. "Let us examine it further!" Your friends are too funny. And obvious!

But you're kind of glad they left you alone. You wouldn't want them to see that all the hairs on your arms are standing up.

"You came!" Jimmy says when you get closer.

"Of course! I wouldn't have missed this for the world."

Jimmy bashfully drops his head and ruffles the back of his hair. "Aw, thanks. I, um, I'm glad you're here. I was really nervous before you showed up. But what did you do? Bring the whole school with you?"

You glance around and see a lot of the same people who were at the choir audition, milling around and munching on cubes of cheese. "Who, them? Not my doing. They must have heard about the up-and-coming artist in town and wanted to see for themselves. You can blame me for those two knuckleheads, though." You point out Jessie and Lena mimicking the movements of the performance artist in the other room, who you think is pretending to walk against the wind.

Jimmy laughs again, and you can feel the tension drain out of him. "Did I mention that I'm glad you're here?"

"You did." You smile at him, showing all your teeth. "So, how about giving me a guided tour of your work?"

"I'd be delighted," Jimmy answers in a formal tone, holding out his arm to show you the way.

And as he walks you through his paintings, he impresses you more and more. You knew that Jimmy was talented, but you had no idea *how* talented! Some of the paintings are portraits of his family and his house. Some are landscapes. He even sketched a few superheroes that look even better than they do in the comic books.

"Wow, Jimmy. These are insanely good! Promise me you'll still talk to me when you're a big famous artist and your work is hanging in museums all over the world."

Jimmy chuckles shyly. "Of course we'll still talk. You can be my limo driver or something."

"Ha-ha. Very funny." You give him a soft shove. "But seriously, these are amazing. I'm really proud of you."

He gives you a grateful smile. "Thanks. I'm kinda proud of me too. I can't believe I pulled it off. I even finished the piece I was working on at school."

"No way. Where is it?" you ask, scanning the wall.

"Over here," he says, nodding to where a painting is resting on an easel covered with a cloth. "I wanted you to be the first one to see it."

He pulls back the cover, and the artwork underneath is even better than you could have imagined. It's an oil painting of you, Jimmy, Lena, Jessie, Charlie, Jasmine, Lizette, Celia and Delia, and even Holly and Mary, hanging out in the lunchroom. There's so much detail! You can see Holly rolling her eyes, you can make out three of Jessie's silver bangles, and you can even read Jimmy's "Picasso Is My Homeboy" T-shirt. Beneath the painting, a small plaque attached to the easel states:

The Indefinables
Artist: James Morehouse
12 years old

Since you are absolutely speechless, you can't think of anything else to do but reach over and hug Jimmy for the first time. The day at school wasn't exactly perfect (understatement alert), but you're more than happy to put that behind you now and just enjoy the moment. Life, sometimes, can be very, very cool.

THE END

chapter
TWENTY-ONE

If it's new, it's for you! You like to keep life interesting. So there's nothing you love better than discovering something new and different. Doing the same-old-same-old all the time can get . . . well, old. So whenever you have the chance, you shake things up—whether it's by getting the latest hairstyle, exploring a different neighborhood, or just eating at a restaurant you've never heard of. Because you aren't afraid to experience new things, life will never be boring. Just remember: Some things, like friendships, get better with age.

If your friends had told you this morning that you would be ending the day by playing miniature golf with Joey Cruz, one of the most popular guys in school, you would have told them they were crazy. You would have thought that minigolf was too cheesy for a jock like him.

198

But here you are, at a course right by the school, and you're having a better time than you thought you would. You've actually always wanted to come here, but it's kind of a cool-kid hangout, and up until now you were too intimidated to enter their turf. With Joey by your side, though, you almost feel like you belong. Besides, you're enjoying a bit of newfound popularity thanks to your stellar performance at the choir auditions. People who have never even spoken to you before are stopping to congratulate you as they pass you on the course.

"Dude, nice going," Eli Santini says as he walks by with Shawna. He's so tall that he has to bend over a little to lean on his putter. "You've got some pipes on you."

"Um, thanks." After you get over the initial surprise of Eli speaking to you, you ask, "But weren't you rooting for Mona?"

"Oh, you mean because I played the piano for her during her audition?" He waves that away with one lanky arm. "Nah, I just like playing the piano—doesn't really matter who for. I was kinda hoping somebody would knock her off her high horse."

"Eli!" Shawna exclaims, playfully slapping his arm. "That's not very nice."

"But it's true. I heard she even refused to be in the choir if she couldn't have the solo. Gimme a break. Besides, you didn't vote for her either."

Shawna blushes a little. "Yeah, well . . . I had to vote for the one who deserved it the most." Shawna winks at you, says congratulations, and then leads Eli over to the next hole.

"Wow," Joey says after they leave, appraising you with his caramel eyes. "I feel like I'm golfing with a celebrity! Autograph seekers might mob you any minute. You're probably too famous to even play minigolf here, yeah?"

"Bite your tongue! If being famous means never getting to putt a ball through a giant windmill, then I'll never sing again!"

"Oh, but you can't do that," Joey replies. "I mean, what about your fans? They'd be crushed." When he smiles you notice his row of crooked teeth and how white they are against the deep tan of his skin. Cute. Very cute.

"Yeah, you're right. Maybe I'll just build my own miniature golf course behind my mansion." You putt your small red ball down the slope, where it dips right into the clown's mouth and comes out the other side, landing inches away from the hole.

"Nice," Joey observes, taking his own shot. "I hope you'll invite me over to your mansion sometime. You know, if I'm not too busy winning the World Series."

"Is that what you want to do? Play professional baseball?" you ask as you putt your ball into the hole.

"It would be cool," Joey admits. "But if that doesn't work out, well . . . don't laugh. But because of Mrs. O'Donnell, I've kind of been thinking about being a librarian or maybe a writer. I'm pretty good at computers too. Maybe being a graphic artist would be fun. . . ."

As soon as the word "artist" comes out of his mouth, you feel a pang of guilt in your belly. You had planned to spend only a little while with Joey and then head off to the community center to see Jimmy, but you started having so much fun (and, okay, basking in everyone's adoration) that you lost track of time. It's been so cool getting to know Joey, but just thinking about Jimmy nervously hanging his paintings makes you want to head over there immediately.

"Um, Joey? I really hate to putt and run, but I have somewhere I need to be."

Joey looks up, confused. "What—now? But we haven't even made it to the waterfall yet."

"I know. . . . And I hate bailing on you, but, well, you know Jimmy Morehouse?"

Joey squints as he searches his mental Rolodex. "The art kid who always has paint on his clothes and untied shoelaces?"

You smile at the sweet image. "That's the one. Well, he's in an art show at the community center and I promised I would go."

Joey scratches his prominent chin. "Uh-huh, I see. Sooo . . . you like him or something?"

Wow. It's been a while since anyone asked you point-blank like that. Is your crush that obvious? "Um . . . well, he . . . I mean, we . . ." You trail off before finally saying, "We're friends."

"Right," Joey says, nodding knowingly. You think he

looks just a little disappointed too. "Well, I understand. Maybe another time?"

"Definitely," you say, smiling as you hand him your putter and the scorecard. "You were beating me anyway."

As you turn to leave, Joey touches your hand and says, "If you change your mind, I'll be right here, probably trying to dig my way out of the sand trap."

You grin. "I'll keep that in mind." As you walk away you speed dial Jessie and Lena and tell them to meet up with you. They won't want to miss this.

So you got to know someone new, and it turned out to be pretty fun! Joey is far from the too-cool-for-you jock you thought he was. He's actually kind and smart and likes the same cheesy stuff you do. Who knew? It just goes to show that you can't judge a book by its cover. You're so flattered by all the attention you're getting that you're tempted to stay right there with Joey. But your heart says there's somewhere you'd rather be.

QUIZ TIME!

Come on, don't you know yourself well enough by now? There's only one place you want to be. So get over to page 193, and make it fast.

chapter
TWENTY-TWO

In your humble opinion, if you want something done right, you have to do it yourself. That's fine when it comes to homework and chores. But when you start trying to control your friends and family, you might hit a few roadblocks. Ruling the universe is a lot of responsibility! It may be scary, but once you realize that you can't control everything, you'll be a lot less stressed. There's a certain freedom in taking life as it comes.

As you sit there in the locker room, those last moments with Jessie play over and over again in your mind. What was that about? She just flitted away with those popular girls as if it was no big deal. Well, it's a big deal to you, and if she thinks you're going to stand by while she be-comes one of them, she'll have to think again!

You throw on your jeans and T-shirt, and instead of going directly to your next class head right for the music room, where Jessie said she'd be practicing with her new "friends." In minutes you're standing outside the door, fully expecting to catch them hanging out and goofing off. Be-fore long, she'll be sitting at their lunch table instead of yours. She might even do the unthinkable and (gasp) start hanging out with Mona! It's high time you take this whole Jessie-and-the-in-crowd thing into your own hands.

But when you barge in, the scene is actually pretty inno-cent. Eli Santini is sitting at the piano, playing different chords; Shawna, Steven, and Adam are rifling through the costume bin from the last theater club's production of *Xanadu;* and Dionne is sitting on the choir bleachers listen-ing to an iPod and taking notes.

And in the middle of all this is Jessie, standing next to Kevin at the piano happily singing scales. Okay, so she really is practicing for the audition. But does she have to do it with them? You can tell that if you don't do something, you'll lose Jessie to this crowd forever.

"What's going on here?" you shout over all the noise.

"La-la-la-la-la—hey! What are you doing here?" Jessie shouts, interrupting her scales to wave at you.

"Saving you," you say dramatically. (Never let it be said that you don't know how to bring the drama.) You cross your arms and narrow your eyes as you look at all these . . . best-friend stealers.

Jessie looks big-time confused. "Um, saving me? From what?"

"From them!" you shout, gesturing to everyone around you. "They're only being nice to you now because they think you might get the solo spot and be worthy of their little clique. But why haven't they spoken to you all this time, huh? Have you forgotten that up until today, they didn't consider you cool enough to be seen with?"

Shawna seems genuinely offended. "What are you talking about?" she says incredulously. "Jessie came to my birthday party last summer, remember?"

"Yeah, but only because Lena won a ticket and took her along, not because Jessie was actually invited," you snap. Okay, that is technically true, but bringing it up is unnecessarily cruel. You can see the shame all over Jessie's face, but you can't seem to stop yourself.

"And what about in third grade when we went on that school trip and you wouldn't let Jessie sit with you guys on the bus? Or how about when you had that Halloween party when we were eight and you didn't invite either one of us, huh? How about that?" Yes, all those incidents are ancient history, but why should that matter? If they did those things to Jessie back then, they might treat her that way again now. You're not letting them off the hook.

Even though you're taking this very seriously, Dionne

laughs as if she can't believe her ears. "Are you for real? You're still holding a grudge over stuff that happened when we were eight?"

Adam doesn't say a word but whistles and makes the "cuckoo" sign with his finger, getting another big laugh from Dionne and Shawna.

Jessie, on the other hand, is completely silent, clearly too mortified to utter a single word. Instead, she gathers up her backpack, looks at you with tears welling in her eyes, and runs out of the room.

"Smooth move, genius," Eli says after Jessie's exit, continuing to tinkle the piano keys.

"Y-y-yeah," Kevin adds, your irrational outburst bringing out his stutter. "D-did it ever occur to y-you that we were hanging with Jessie 'cause we think she's c-c-c . . ." He shakes his head. ". . . awesome?"

You try to hold on to your hostility, which for some reason you thought was totally justified a few moments ago. But now, with all these kids looking at you as if you have two heads, you feel . . . well, pretty silly.

Tsk, tsk, tsk. . . . It would be nice if you could convince yourself that you just did Jessie a favor, but you know better. That whole outburst wasn't for her sake, but for yours. You saw her making new friends and you wanted to force her not to. But the only thing your control-freak maneuver accomplished was to make Jessie not want to be your friend anymore. And can you blame her? You embarrassed her in front of some of the most popular kids in school (who were only trying to help her, by the way), and you made yourself look like a lunatic. You need to do some major damage control if you hope to salvage your friendship.

QUIZ TIME!

Oh, you wish you could take a quiz to get out of this. But there's no escaping what you have to do. Go to page 161 to apologize to Jessie.

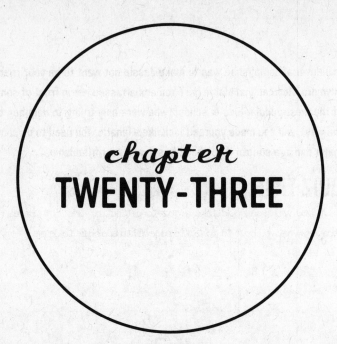

chapter
TWENTY-THREE

Peer pressure is no match for you. Sure, your friends occasionally try to talk you into doing things you don't want to do, but you have mastered the fine art of saying no. As a result, you live life on your own terms and don't bow to anyone's wishes but your own. What you may want to open yourself up to, though, is *positive* peer pressure. If your friends encourage you to do better in school when you've been goofing off, for example, or to seek help when you have a major problem, that kind of pressure can be a lifesaver.

As far as you know, you don't have asthma, but you sure are finding it hard to breathe. Maybe that's because, as Mona comes to the stage, you are crossing all your fingers and toes and wishing as hard as you can that she'll be as terrible as her personality.

Too bad crossing your toes never works when it really counts. After announcing her name and her song choice—"Party in the USA" by Miley Cyrus—Mona takes the microphone off the stand and launches into the song. And you are sorely disappointed to hear that she's not bad. Actually, she's pretty good. Her voice is perfect for the up-tempo hit, and she even works the stage like a pro. When she gets to the part where she sings "I put my hands up, they're playing my song," a bunch of kids in the audience put their hands up too and start dancing along. Say what you will about Mona, but she definitely knows how to perform. When she finishes, she slides the microphone back into the stand in one smooth movement and bows to the crowd. She steps off the stage with loud applause trailing after her.

It's a hard act to follow. And unfortunately, Jessie is up next. You know it's useless, but you cross your fingers and toes again, this time hoping that Jessie rocks it.

"I'm Jessie Miller and I'll be singing 'Seven Things' by Miley Cyrus." She gives you a nervous smile and you flash back a thumbs-up. *You can do it!* you shout in your mind, just in case she can read it.

And it's a miracle, but the toe-crossing actually works! As Jessie starts singing about the seven things she hates about an unnamed "you," you are relieved to hear that she doesn't sound anywhere near as bad as she did this morning. She might not make it to the finals on *American Idol*, but she would at least make it past the first round. Phew! You're thrilled for her, and clap wildly when she's done.

But before you get too caught up in the celebration, Lisa nudges you with her elbow and whispers, "Don't forget what we talked about earlier." Oh, how you wish you could. While most of the judges are clapping and smiling at Jessie, Maria and Lisa are looking right at you with intense stares. Sheesh! It's like they've had intimidation training or something. Next thing you know they'll whip out a ceiling light with one bare bulb in it and point it at your face.

Shaking the image away, you look into the audience instead, finding Lena and Charlie sitting a few rows back from the stage. After Jessie takes her seat next to them, all three smile confidently at you. Argh . . . you know that your pals expect you to vote for Jessie. But they have no idea that Lisa is holding a loaded elbow to your rib cage. What to do? What to do?

As you start to give in to the early stages of a first-class freak-out, Jasmine Viera takes the stage. You've never heard her sing before, but judging from her fairly quiet speaking voice, you doubt she'll be able to contend with Mona.

She announces that she chose "Apologize" by One Republic, opens her mouth, and the most beautiful voice you've ever heard in real life comes out. OMG! How many times can you be dead wrong today? It's like you're going for a record or something. Did you actually just think that Jasmine wouldn't be able to compete with Mona? Wow, you were *way* off! As she sings the very high "It's tooo laaaaate," Jasmine's voice is smooth and sweet, lingering easily over the high-pitched note. She even uses a little vibrato, deepening the sound.

Bottom line? She's fantastic. No one could deny that she is soloist material. Even Mona's light blue eyes are opened wide in amazement.

After a few more auditions (none of them as impressive as Jasmine's), Mr. Parker gives the judges a few minutes to vote. When it comes time to reveal the outcomes, the voting is all over the place.

A few of the teachers vote for Jessie, saying that they like her attitude. Jessie breaks into a huge smile. Most of the others vote for Jasmine. But when the student judges all vote for Mona, the score is tied. And guess who gets the tiebreaking vote? Yep. That would be you. Everyone in the room seems to be holding their breath, waiting to see what you'll do.

You know that you're going to let down some people — and probably add to your list of people who hate you from the popular clique — but you have to do the right thing. You hold up your ballot so that Mr. Parker can see it. "I voted for Jasmine."

There is an uproar as the room fills with thunderous applause. Jasmine takes the soloist spot! She is an instant celebrity, which must be weird for someone who's used to getting that kind of attention only from teachers. Good for her! Your friends and the mean-girl duo look equally shocked.

"That was really stupid," Maria hisses at you.

"Yeah, you blew it," Lisa insists.

But you just shake your head as if you pity them. "No, *you* blew it. No one bosses me around. But *your* boss looks pretty mad," you say, nodding at Mona, whose porcelain face is red with rage. "She already hated me before, so it's no biggie. But you guys probably have a rough year ahead, am I right?"

The two of them look in Mona's direction and wilt in their seats. "Great," Lisa says miserably.

Yes, it is pretty great.

When you finally find your friends in the midst of the crowd of kids who are still milling around, congratulating Jasmine and all the others who made it into the choir, you aren't sure if they're going to hug you or bite your head off.

"Um, hey, guys," you say uncertainly. "Mind if I join you?"

"Of course!" Jessie shouts, pulling you in for a tight squeeze.

"Wait . . . you're not mad?" you ask her. "I thought for sure you'd hate me forever for voting for Jasmine over you."

Jess curls her fists and plants them on her hips. It's her classic "You're being a blockhead" move. "Come on, gimme a little credit, will ya? Even I can see that Jasmine totally deserved it. Who knew that beneath that teacher's-pet surface lurked a musical genius?"

You breathe out in relief, releasing all the tension you've been holding in for the past few hours.

"I know, right? And did you see Mona's face? I think her head might explode!" you say.

Your friends giggle a little. "If she thinks this was bad," Lena says, "just wait until she reads about it all over again in our blog!"

Charlie beams proudly. "It's our best work yet, if I do say so myself."

Just then you see Melanie and Kevin coming toward you. Both of them used to be good friends of yours when you were little. But over the years you've ended up on different sides of the social fence. "Hey," Melanie cuts in, patting you on the back. Kevin is right behind her, looking at you with what you think is respect in his eyes. "I just wanted to say it was really cool what you did up there, not automatically voting for Mona. A little birdie told me there was some pressure for you to do that." (Your guess? A little birdie = Amy Choi. Somehow that girl knows all!)

"Yeah," Kevin adds. "I'm not sure I would have had the guts."

"Thanks, guys," you say, feeling truly proud of yourself for the first time today. Not only did you hand the victory to the right person, but by standing up to Mona's crew, you have taken a brick out of the wall that is separating the cliques. Feeling like you're on a roll, you decide to see if you can take out a few more.

"Listen, if you guys aren't doing anything now, would

213

you want to go see an awesome art exhibit at the community center? Our very own Jimmy Morehouse is showing
his paintings and it's sure to be even cooler than this audition was."

You know they wouldn't normally go to anything that
wasn't clique-approved, but right now they're open to it.
Melanie shrugs. "Sure, sounds like fun. Mind if I invite
people?"

"Not at all!" you exclaim. "In fact, invite everybody. No
one will want to miss this."

When Melanie and Kevin disappear back into the crowd
to start spreading the word, Jessie warns, "Are you sure
that's a good idea? Jimmy looked pretty stressed out
about his show. He might not love it if a million people
show up."

You slide your arm around her shoulders, smiling confidently. "He won't mind if all those people are friends."

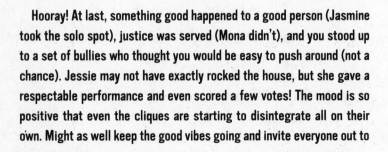

Hooray! At last, something good happened to a good person (Jasmine
took the solo spot), justice was served (Mona didn't), and you stood up
to a set of bullies who thought you would be easy to push around (not a
chance). Jessie may not have exactly rocked the house, but she gave a
respectable performance and even scored a few votes! The mood is so
positive that even the cliques are starting to disintegrate all on their
own. Might as well keep the good vibes going and invite everyone out to

an event that will strengthen your new bonds—and make your heart beat a little faster.

QUIZ TIME!

No time for quizzes now. Your favorite artist awaits! Head over to page 193.

chapter
TWENTY-FOUR

You are one laid-back lady! You don't mind not having control over the whole world. To you, it's much more fun to just let things happen. And since you enjoy your own freedom, you never try to boss other people around. But be careful not to relinquish all control. (Your wreck of a backpack, for example, could probably use a little management!)

You take your seat next to Charlie and Lena in the auditorium, where the auditions are taking place, having absolutely no idea what to expect. You haven't really gotten to talk to Jessie since gym class, so you have no clue how your BFF is feeling, which is unusual for the two of you. Then again, nothing about today has been usual. You're not even sure if she is still your BFF or if she'll forget all about you and Lena and upgrade to Shawna and Dionne.

"Have you talked to Jessie?" you whisper to Lena as the auditions begin. "I mean, where is she? And is she ready for this?"

"Shh," Lena whispers back, holding her caramel-colored index finger over her full lips. "We're trying to listen. This is the big finale for the blog."

You stop talking for a minute, then anxiously lean over again. "But seriously, what's going on with her?"

"Shh," Lena repeats. "You'll find out soon enough."

Ugh. You hate it when Lena is cryptic. That means something is going on and everybody knows it but you. You can barely sit still through the barrage of hopefuls grabbing the mike. But finally something happens to take your mind off Jessie temporarily.

Mona Winston takes the stage, looking *Gossip Girl* stylish, of course, in her black leggings, wrap dress, and matching headband. Each strand of her long black hair seems to have been placed there by a professional. Given Mona's modeling connections, maybe they were!

But along with all the fashion-forward clothes, Mona is wearing a smug grin that makes you want to boo her off the stage. If there is any justice in the world, her singing voice will be as sour as her attitude.

Mona grabs the mike and launches into the first stanza of

Miley's "Party in the USA," and that seals it. There is no justice in the world. As much as it kills you to admit it, Mona has some skills. Not only does she have a decent voice, she knows how to work the crowd, getting them to wave their arms back and forth with her when she sings "I put my hands up, they're playing my sooong." You want to hate on her performance, but you just can't—she's good. Bummer.

When she finishes, you begrudgingly clap along with everyone else. Even though she isn't your favorite person, you believe in giving credit where credit is due.

But if you thought Mona was good, you haven't heard anything yet. Jasmine Viera is next to hit the stage, and her version of "Apologize" by One Republic stuns the whole room into silence. Even Mona's conceited grin falters when faced with Jasmine's downright angelic voice. Who knew that a girl who spent so much time being the teacher's pet could sing like that? Like you mentioned before: Today has been anything but usual. She gets even more applause than Mona did. (As you can imagine, Mona isn't pleased.)

As thrilled as you are that Jasmine just smoked Mona's performance, you are now twice as nervous for Jessie. How is she supposed to follow those two and survive? If it were you, you'd be tempted to back out. But you know Jessie has too much backbone to do that. It's one of the things you admire most about her. Even if she has defected to the popular clique, you're still rooting for your friend. But where is she?

Just when you are about to ask Lena again, fully prepared to get shushed for the third time, Jessie Miller enters
the room. There are gasps all over the auditorium as she
bravely walks up to the microphone. Sometime between
when you saw her during gym and right now, Jessie transformed into a total goddess. Her golden blond wavy hair,
which she usually keeps bound up in a high ponytail, is cas-
cading down around her shoulders like a lion's mane. And
instead of the jeans and turtleneck she was wearing earlier,
she is wearing a sparkly purple tank top, a flowing purple
chiffon skirt, and matching knee-high boots. The only part
of her outfit that you recognize from before are the signature bangles jangling around her wrists. For a second
there, you thought Taylor Swift had shown up to audition!

"Wha . . . ?" you gasp. "When did all this happen?"

But Jessie's new glammed-up appearance isn't the only
surprise. Her actual performance ends up being the biggest
shock of all. She is still singing the song you picked out for
her, Miley's "7 Things," but it's the *way* she's singing it. She
may not have the best voice in the room, but she's got real
stage presence! Even without any stage lights on, Jessie
seems to be glowing. And she's kind of acting out the lyrics,
really leaning into some of the notes and giving them life.
By the middle of the song, all the kids (and some of the
teachers) are up on their feet, cheering for her as if this is
a real concert instead of a school audition. Wow. Just . . .
wow!

Needless to say, the applause she gets when she leaves

the stage is deafening, and you aren't the only one to give her a standing ovation. There are even some cries of "Encore! Encore!"

Well, if Jessie wasn't part of the popular crowd before, she certainly will be a candidate now.

After Mr. Parker gives the judges a few minutes to vote, he asks each judge to name their choice for soloist. Jasmine and Mona each get a few votes, but Jessie wins by a landslide! It is the upset of the year! The crowd goes wild, and Jessie is immediately surrounded by what seems like a thousand kids all wanting to congratulate her.

"*Yes!*" Lena yells, jumping to her feet and throwing her journalistic objectivity right out the window. "Woooohoooo! Go, Jessie!"

You are just as excited, but you doubt Jessie is going to come celebrate with you. Look at her. She's practically a celebrity now! Shawna, Dionne, and Adam even push through the crowd to hug her. You figure Jess will probably go off with her new friends afterward to celebrate, so you hang back, feeling . . . well, you're not sure how you feel. Is it possible to be extremely happy and extremely sad at the same time? 'Cause you're so there.

You tell Lena you have to go and start heading for the door. You're almost at the exit when you get tackled from behind.

"Hey! Where do you think you're going?" Jessie yells, squeezing you so hard you can't breathe. "Can you believe it? I won. I won!" She swings you from side to side with a strength that can only come from a huge rush of adrenaline, and you squeal and laugh.

"I know! It's awesome," you finally gasp. "But would you mind letting go now? My face is turning blue."

"Oh!" Jessie lets go right away and then swings you around so that you're facing her. "Sorry, I'm just so excited! I can't believe I won. But I guess between you picking out the perfect song, and Shawna, Dionne, and Adam helping me out with—"

"Wait—they helped you with the audition?"

"Totally!" Jessie gushes. "I wasn't sure they were allowed to, since they're judges and all. But they didn't promise to vote for me or anything. And I think Lisa and some of the other girls actually wanted me to fail. They kept telling me to sing that Taylor Swift song, which I know now was all wrong for me. But Shawna and Dionne told me not to listen to them. They gave me some great performance tips, and then Adam remembered that there was this purple outfit left over from the production of *Xanadu* that might fit me. Letting my hair down was my idea. What do you think?"

"I think Taylor Swift better make way for you! You were amazing! I'm so proud of you."

Jessie bounces up and down excitedly and claps her hands like a little girl. Same old Jessie. So the popular kids really did help her. Maybe they aren't all the monsters you make them out to be.

"Thanks!"

While Charlie goes to interview the other new choir members (Lizette, Jasmine, and Kevin all got in; Mark, not so much), Lena joins you and Taylor—uh, that is, Jessie— for your lovefest. "So did you tell her yet?" Lena asks Jessie.

"What, about Shawna and those guys helping her with the audition? Yeah."

"No, not that. The *other* thing."

There's another thing? You're not sure you can take any more surprises.

"Not yet," Jessie answers with a smile. She claps her hands again and bounces so that her skirt swirls out like a small purple cream puff. "You know Adam, right?" she says to you.

"Duh," you deadpan. "Everybody knows who Adam is."

"Right, well, the reason I ran off after gym wasn't only because I wanted to go practice. Adam wanted to talk to me alone because . . . he likes you! He wants to ask you out to a movie."

Jess is talking so fast right now that you don't catch what she's saying. "Wait, slow down," you beg her. "I can't under-stand you. To me it sounded like you said 'Adam likes you.' But that can't be right."

Jessie squeals again, her blue eyes rounding into saucers. "It is! He said he thought the fact that you told me the truth and picked out a better song was really cool. He's wanted to meet you ever since. I'm not sure if you'll like him or not, but he was even checking you out in gym class. Didn't you notice?"

"Um, no." You were too busy thinking your friendship was ending to realize that Jessie would never do that to you. You turn to Lena. "And you knew about this?"

"I did . . . and it's been killing me to keep it in! But I was sworn to secrecy, and a good journalist knows how to be discreet."

"So, what should I tell him? Do you want to go see a movie with him tonight?" While your friends stare at you, waiting for your answer, Adam himself comes sauntering over.

"Uhh . . . Lena, let's go find Charlie," Jessie spits out quickly. In a flash, they're gone and you're left alone with Adam.

"Hi there," Adam says smoothly, running his hand through his silky blond hair.

"Hi." And there you have it, folks. The first conversation between you and superpopular Adam.

"So, I guess Jessie told you that I'll be taking you to the movies."

"Well, nooo. Jessie told me you'd be *asking* me to the movies."

Adam looks confused for a second. "Yeah, that's what I meant." He fixes the swoop in his hair again with one hand and taps his fingers against his jeans. "So I heard what you did for Jessie. Good looking out."

"Oh, thanks. It's just what any good friend would do."

"It's too bad I didn't know you and her were so cool this whole time. I would have rescued you from your side of the lunchroom a lot sooner."

"Rescued?" you ask, watching him fix his hair yet again.

"Well, yeah, I just mean, most of the kids who sit on your side of the caf are kind of . . ."

"They're kind of awesome," you finish for him. And there you have it, folks! What might be the last conversation between you and superpopular Adam. The kids on your side of the cafeteria might be indefinable misfits, but they're also your friends.

Is it really possible to have a heart attack from too many surprises? If so, someone really ought to get you to a hospital, STAT! First Mona, Jasmine, and of course Jessie blow you away with unexpectedly great auditions. Then you find out that some of the popular girls are not so mean after all. And now you hear that Adam has a thing for you, and Lena knew about it all along? It's too much! You were definitely interested in getting to know Adam better until you realized that he's still a little stuck-up. Hopefully he'll grow out of that. For now, you'd rather spend time with someone who really understands you.

QUIZ TIME!

No need for a quiz. Anybody who knows you (and that should include you by now) knows where you're heading next. So fly over to page 193.

Crystal Velasquez is the author of four books in the Maya & Miguel series —*My Twin Brother/My Twin Sister, Neighborhood Friends, The Valentine Machine,* and *Paint the Town* —and *Your Life, but Better!,* her first book for older readers. She holds a bachelor's degree in creative writing from Pennsylvania State University and is a graduate of the New York University Summer Publishing Institute. Currently a production editor and a freelance proofreader, she lives in Flushing, Queens, in New York City. Visit the author's Web site at www.crystalvelasquez.com.